PENALTY KICKS

A Good Samaritan Mystery

By

James M. Courneya

TABLE OF CONTENTS

THE PLOT BEGINS

The older Plymouth Reliant moved slowly down Railroad Ave. It was a smoker. The sedan seemed to be choking out its last breaths, maybe it was. The Plymouth had no discernible color. Most of the paint had washed away from the years of sitting outside in the wet Washington weather. The car slowed as it came up to the railroad crossing making a complete stop in the middle of the tracks. Killing the engine as a man climbed out, he stopped to lock the door. An off-white Dodge panel van pulled up to the crossing. The man climbed into the passenger side of the van.

"Jesus, you took forever to get here. I drove around the neighborhood three times."

"It wasn't my fault. That damn car died at least every other block. Boy, if that's the car that saved Chrysler, maybe they should have let them die."

"You know we needed an old car that no one could trace to us, so just live with it."

"Is the scanner working?" Just then the scanner started talking. It was tuned into the railroad radio channels.

"Does that answer your question?" The men rode in silence for a few minutes. The route the van driver took was around the large rail yard located in the southern part of Auburn.

"Watch for the access road. It should be coming up." Both men saw the access road at the same time.

"Cut your lights, we've gone too far to be stopped because of headlights." The night was clear, so driving through the end of the yard to their destination was uneventful. A small stub track contained a string of boxcars. They stopped, after pulling up alongside the third boxcar.

"Hey Arnie, what are you gonna do after we tie up?"

"Same old thing, the better half is expecting me early because we go on vacation starting Friday."

"Robin, what's that at the crossing?" Arnie started blowing the locomotive's horn.

"It's a car and it ain't moving." Both men braced themselves as Arnie placed the train in emergency. Arnie kept blowing the horn, but the car never moved. The train didn't stop in time to avoid hitting the car. The lead engine impacted the car in a sickening crush of steel on steel. The car was cut in half with the impact. The train rolled to a stop almost a block down the tracks from the crossing.

"Cascade and Pacific' s Ellensburg Turn calling East Auburn Dispatcher."

"East Auburn Dispatcher answering the Ellensburg Turn."

"Bob, we've hit a car at the Valley Rd. crossing. The train is stopped. I don't know if the car was occupied. Send emergency personnel and company officials."

"They are already on the way. Are you sure that you guys are okay?"

"We're okay, just a little shook up. It's not my first crossing accident and it probably won't be my last one."

"Hold tight, the cavalry's coming. East Auburn Dispatcher, out."

"That's our cue. I'll get the lock off and the door open." The van driver had the lock off the boxcar and the door slid open.

"Here's the list of containers we need to grab." The men took a few moments locating the six containers. The boxes were quickly loaded into the van. The door was moved back to look like it was closed. The men drove the van out of the yard heading south out of town. This all took less than ten minutes.

Mac Delac caught the call for the crossing accident. Even the Special Agent in Charge had to cover after hour calls. Railroads for the most part operated 24/7. Mac pulled up to the Valley Road crossing and turned his caution lights on. Fuzees and cones had been placed on each side of the crossing. The local police were already on the scene rerouting cars around the accident scene in both directions. Mac walked up the track towards the locomotives.

"Hey Arnie, are you and Robin okay?"

"Yeah we're fine, but I'm gonna be in big trouble at home for being late, though."

"Sorry, but you know the drill, the trainmaster will be here shortly, after that you get to pee in a cup. Let's see what we have, okay." Mac started looking at the remains of the car. Using his flashlight Mac looked inside both halves of the vehicle. The car looked very clean. No sign of blood or occupants in fact, the interior looked as if no one had ever been inside. The Special Agent on duty had been on another call, so he was just now pulling up. Joe Frederick was the youngest of the Cascade and Pacific special agents. Joe mostly worked nights. Mac considered Joe a very good agent.

"Mac, what do you want me to do?"

"Joe, we need to walk both sides of the track from here to the crossing. I haven't pulled the cameras yet, so we'll do that when we get done working the ground."

"Let me grab my light and an evidence bag before we get started."

It was morning before all the accident work was done. The camera and tapes would be processed by the railroads contract lab. The crew had been tested, gave their statements before the trainmaster took them back to the terminal to log off the job. A new crew was waiting for the mechanical guys to give the okay to move the train the last mile into the yard. Mac then headed back to his office to finish his paperwork and brief the day shift agents before being able to go home and sleep.

THE NEW TEACHER

Joey Simone made his way to his sixth period Contemporary American History class. The hall was swarming with students hustling to get to their classes on time. Joey wasn't sure what to expect because his class was being taught by a new teacher. A group of friends waited for Joey outside the door to the sixth period class.

"Joey, what took you so long?" Paul Toomey smacked Joey as he asked his question.

"I took a long shower after P.E. We were running the track and I worked up a good stink. I didn't want to make a bad impression on the new teacher."

"You've always been a suck-up. You still smell." Everyone laughed at Joey and headed into the class to find seats. The guys found seats towards the back of the room. A younger man came into the room and shut the door. The athletic looking man was dressed casually for a teacher. The students quieted down waiting for class to start. In a few swift strokes the man wrote his name on the wipe-board; Tad Shipley.

"Good afternoon, I'm Tad Shipley, and this is Contemporary American History. I like to spend the first day of class getting to know my students and sharing a little of my background with you. I was raised in Auburn. My family still lives there. I played soccer in high school and at Highline College. I'm still a big fan.

After my years at Highline, I joined the Army, mostly because I needed a break from school, after enlisting I spent four years in the military. By the time that I got out of the service I was ready to go back to school. Western Washington was my choice to finish my degree. I've been a teacher for five years. Any questions, so far?"

"What did you do in the Army?" Bob Jensen asked. Bob has been talking about joining the Army for as long as anyone can remember.

"Believe it or not, I drove tanks."

"That's so cool." Bob was in love.

"Since you've already joined the conversation, why don't you tell us a little about yourself, starting with your name, okay?" Bob gave a very short bio about himself.

The students all gave little bits and pieces about themselves. The class had worked its way from the front towards the back. Joey Simone was the last student to go.

"You in the back give us your story."

Joey stood up and started, "My name is Joey Simone. I'm a twelve-year senior."

Mr. Shipley interrupted Joey. "Wait a minute, what's a twelve-year senior?"

"Here at Twin Rivers, a student that has gone from kindergarten through 12th grade is called a twelve-year senior. You get honored at graduation for being one."

"That's kind of cool, what did you say your name is?"

"Joey Simone."

"Are you related to the Simone's from Auburn?"

"Yes, I have a lot of relatives in Auburn."

"I played soccer for a coach named Simone, I think his name was Sam. Do you know him?"

"He's my dad." Mr. Shipley was all smiles as Joey told him.

"Your dad was my favorite coach growing up. Tell him that I said hi."

"I will." The bell rang announcing the end of the class and the school day. There was a loud rush to the door. Joey and his friends headed to their lockers.

"Joey are you going to hang around and watch the baseball game?"

"Just for a few innings. I've got some stuff to do this afternoon."

"We'll meet you there in a few minutes. Do you want anything from the store?"

"Get me a Big Gulp. Toomes owes me five bucks."

"Bob owes you more than that, make him pay."

"You two figure it out, okay." Bob and Toomey sped off to 7/11 to get some goodies. Joey put his books in his locker and closed the door. That's when he spotted Ginger Brown standing by the exit to the ball fields. Joey had been hoping to catch up with Ginger. Joey couldn't keep his mind off Ginger. She kept him awake at night. Ginger was a long-legged, auburn haired beauty. Joey shared about half his classes with her. Joey had known Ginger since kindergarten. Joey had other crushes before, but this felt different somehow. On shaky legs, Joey approached the woman of his desires.

"Hi Joey, are you going to the baseball game?" God, what a voice, the voice of an angel.

"Yeah, do you want to sit together?" Joey felt like his whole future depended on her answer.

"I was hoping you'd ask." Ginger gave Joey a smile that almost set his hair on fire. Joey reached out and took Ginger's hand. The happiest man on earth walked his lady to the bleachers.

Joey and Ginger were just getting settled when Bob and Toomey arrived with their haul from 7/11. They handed out the goodies and sat down noisily next to Joey.

The teams were warming up waiting for the game to start. Bob and Toomey didn't have a clue that something had changed in their world order, but Joey holding hands with Ginger was a major shift for these guys.

"Ginger, I didn't know that you liked baseball." Toomes asked.

"I'm not a big fan of baseball, but I like to support our school."

"I hear that we might have a really good team this year." Bob added.

"Who told you that? We suck at most sports except girls' soccer and that's only because Marie is such a good player." Toomes liked Marie, but she never gave him any encouragement.

"Wait a minute, we finished with a winning record in football this year."

"You just proved my point, Joey, that was the first winning season in the last decade."

"Guys, the game is about to start, why don't we watch and see if they're any good?" Ginger added.

The batter from Elk River stepped into the batter's box and waited for the first pitch. Jumpin' Johnny Jones went into his windup and sent the first pitch of the season and game towards home plate.

"Strike." The umpire roared as the fastball slammed into Squatty Brown's catcher's mitt. Squatty threw a strike back to Johnny. The game was a low scoring affair until the fifth inning when Twin River managed to put runners on first and second. Squatty Brown ambled up to the plate. The runners took their leads and Elk River's pitcher stepped off the rubber and looked hesitant about what to do.

"Time," shouted Elk River's coach and everyone relaxed as the coach went to the mound and tried to calm down his young pitcher.

"If Squatty can get a hit it might break the game open."

"Joey, you know that this is where our guy always hits into a triple play." Toomes was the most vocal non-supporter of all their classmates. Toomes loved to cheer for the visiting team in the student section. The other kids would throw popcorn and garbage at him. Toomes always had a big grin on his face when he got his friends and classmates to react to his negative comments.

The coach finished giving the pitcher his expert advice and started back to the first base dugout. Just as the coach was sitting down, the now re-energized hurler sent his fastball towards Squatty. Squatty wiggled his bat before it made a violent collision with the ball sending it into orbit. The ball crashed off the right-centerfield fence. The long hit scored both runners. Meanwhile, Squatty was standing on second base with a double.

"When was the last time that any one of our guys came through in the clutch?" Toomes was excited as he asked his question.

"It's just the first game. Let's see how the rest of the game and season goes."

"Just wait, you'll see that I'm right. You're all just doubters."

"You might be right, that was a clutch hit. It might just turn into a big rally." We all turned around to see who had joined our conversation. It was the new teacher, Mr. Shipley.

"Wow, we don't get many teachers at ball games."

"I figure that one way to get to know a school is to participate in its activities."

"That's cool. Are you gonna coach or advise any clubs?"

"Well, Joey, I might get involved with soccer. I understand that there's an opening for an assistant-coach."

"You'd get to coach my sister, Marie."

"That would be nice, I could pay-back your dad for coaching me." As we were talking the baseball team began piling up hits and runs, yes, it was a genuine rally against the team that was the preseason favorites to win the league title. The group spent the rest of the game watching their guys look like champs. After the last out, Joey walked Ginger back to her car.

"Ginger would you like to go to the movies with me on Friday?" Joey was sweating as he asked Ginger out. He had never asked anyone out before.

"Sure, Joey, call me with the details later in the week. Here's my number." Ginger hugged Joey and bounced into her car. Joey was floating as he caught up with his buddies.

"Look at Joey, he must have finally done it. You did do it, didn't you?"

"Joey asked Ginger out." All the guys were razzing him and giving him their version of way-to-go. None of Joey's group of friends were what you would call successful around girls, but Joey taking the gigantic step of asking out a girl was a big deal to all of them. The guys talked for a few more minutes before each one headed home. Joey was the last to leave because he had to wait for his sister Marie. Marie was always working out, practicing, or volunteering for school projects. Joey wasn't sure what Marie was doing today, just that she was running a little late.

AN OLD NEMESIS

"Sorry I'm so late, but the planning committee meeting ran really long today. How was the game?"

"We won 8-2. The team looked good."

"What's wrong? You look different. Who'd you sit with?"

"Bob and Toomes and Ginger. The new teacher came over and sat with us for a few innings, too!"

"Ginger, that explains it. My big brother's in love." Marie giggled and slugged Joey.

"I'm not in love, just like. And for your information I asked her out and she said yes."

"I'm impressed. You did this all on your own, wow, I guess we can stop worrying about you. Dad was looking into building a basement for you to live in."

"Did you borrow dad's sense of humor? That's as bad as anything he says." Joey and Marie both laughed as they drove home.

"You guys are running a little late, dinner is almost ready, so wash up and set the table." The smell of spaghetti sauce filled the air. Sam was on dinner duty tonight. Jude got home after Sam two nights a week. On those nights Sam made or bought dinner. Spaghetti has always been Sam's signature dish. Sam learned to cook from his mom. Anna Simone was a great cook. She passed down to her kids the basics of her cooking skills, but she never gave them all of her secrets. Sam's sister Maria had been promised her mother's special cookbook, but when the time came the family found out that Anna's special cookbook was in her head. Maria would visit her mother and help with the cooking, but when she tried making the recipes, they never tasted quite the same.

"Marie, make sure that David gets cleaned up, please."

"I already did that. Do you need help bringing the food out?"

"That would be great, Jude should be here any moment. Add an extra plate, Mac is coming over for dinner."

"Why's Mac coming over, dad?"

"We're playing in that tournament this weekend, so I want to make sure that he has all the information about times and places."

"Mac knows his soccer. I wonder where he learned it from."

"You're a riot, Marie. I bet that I haven't gotten through one day in the last six months without you or your brother busting my chops."

"Oh Dad, I love you, I know that Mac played for you on your first great team, but after this year we'll be your great team." Marie was grinning as she said this.

Mac Delac is Sam's cousin. He's about ten years younger than Sam. His mom, Carmela, is Sam's dad's sister. She married Jimmie Delac. The Delacs are of French-Canadian extraction. I used to tease Mac about being only half Italian. When he was little it would get him, all steamed up. He'd start chasing me trying to smack me, but I could outrun him at least until I hurt my leg in high school. I stopped teasing him after the first time he caught up to me and gave me a swat in the back. It stung pretty darn hard even though I pretended it didn't hurt a bit. It made me retire from teasing my favorite cousin. The Delacs and Simones played at Auburn High School for the best part of ten years. There were three Simones and one Delac when I played. Mac was the last of the line. I coached his club team and now he helps coach Marie's team.

"Who says Mac's team was my first great team? I don't know if I've ever told you about my team that went undefeated in high school."

"Only a thousand times, old man, undefeated, third in state, records that still haven't been broken, but you still can't catch me."

"That's it. No more Al Bundy high school stories. Set the table and we'll eat as soon as Mac shows up." Jude wasn't a lifetime soccer fan, so she sometimes has to bring us back to reality.

"Yes, ma'am!" The doorbell rang saving us from the wrath of my non-soccer loving wife.

"Dad, Mac's here." David yelled from the front door.

"Let him in, David."

"Ok, Daddio."

All of us were soon settled around the table enjoying the meal. It was usually quiet for a few minutes when I served Italian food. Salad, spaghetti, and bread quickly disappeared from the table. Feelings of warmth and contentment filled the room and our belly's. Since I've never been much of a wine drinker, I didn't serve it except on special occasions. Tonight, was a school night not a holiday, so no wine adorned the table and I hadn't made dessert either. The family would just have to settle for some conversation as our after-dinner treat.

"I will be able to make it to the tournament. Unless something tragic happens between now and Saturday." Mac is the Special Agent in Charge, for the Cascade and Pacific Railroad. He's the third generation of his family to work for the railroad. Little Jimmie, Mac's dad, works in the mechanical department, his grandfather, Jimmie Mac, used to be a telephone lineman for them. Mac recently moved in with Jimmie Mac. Mac makes sure that Jimmie Mac is eating right as well as taking care of his-self. I'm not sure Jimmie Mac needs watching. I bet he outlives all of us. Jimmie Mac signed over his house to Mac. Mac is his one and only grandkid. Mac' parents, Little Jimmie and Aunt Carmela own a nice place a few blocks from Jimmie Mac's house.

"That's great, we need all the eyes we can to see what the team needs to work on. The tournament will be a good way to gauge how ready we are."

"They'll be fine. This is a good group of players. I'd say that they're real close to where my old team was at this same age."

"Good God, don't tell any of them that, especially, Marie." That got a laugh out of Mac. Marie is always after me to tell her where she stands among the soccer players of the family. Marie already has enough confidence in her ability, but the truth is that it's hard to compare all the ones that I played with to Marie because I don't want to slight anyone especially my daughter.

"Don't tell me what, dad?"

"Nothing, it's not any of your business."

"Someone must have complimented my soccer ability." Marie had a big grin on her face. "That's okay, I'll just prove it on the field."

"I've been waiting for that for nearly ten years."

"Are you feeling frisky? Jude, dad's getting frisky, you better watch out."

"Marie leave your dad alone. He's getting kind of old and cranky." Jude was always quick to join the nightly pick on the old guy game.

"Where is the tournament at?"

"It's at the new complex in Alpac. They built four new turf fields right off the freeway."

"God, remember how bad the fields were when you coached me?"

"Pretty much cow pastures with chalk lines. The Alpac Soccer Club has come a long way since you lived and played there. They even changed the name of the club to Alpac Youth Soccer."

"Mac, you played in Alpac? I thought you went to Auburn."

"Before my mom and dad bought the house in Auburn, we lived in Alpac. I went to Alpac schools into middle school. I played most of my club career over there. That's where your dad started coaching."

"I have good and bad memories of coaching there. Both teams that I coached were pretty good, but the club was very political which caused some problems along the way. I almost quit coaching because of the problems, but the kids talked me into returning. It worked out fairly well for all of us."

"What do you mean, both teams? I thought that you coached Mac all the way into high school." Marie's question left me uncertain on what to say or do. I haven't talked about getting asked to step down as the coach for years. Mac came to my rescue.

"It's a long story, but probably better to be told on another night."

"Okay Mac, I'm going to hold you to that. I have some homework to finish, so I'll say my good nights. Goodnight everyone."

"Goodnight, Marie."

"You've never told her about coaching in Alpac."

"No, for the most part I don't talk about that at all."

"Honey, was it something bad?" Jude had been listening to the conversation.

"No, it wasn't anything bad at least not on my part, but it made me as mad as I've ever been. I was told that my services were no longer needed because of the issues that boiled over during the season between myself and the other coaches on the team."

"You had other coaches. Wasn't Mac the first assistant coach you've ever had."

"The club forced us to coach together. I never had any other coaches before or after until I asked Mac to help with this team."

"Sam had been coaching my team for about five years when the soccer club told him that they were merging the two teams in our age group. The club said that we didn't have enough players, but we had a full roster, so the club transferred a couple of our kids to an older team and put the rest of us on the Bootlegger's roster. The club president called Sam and told him about the changes just two weeks before the start of the season. Sam was to be one of the assistant coaches. God, he was pretty mad about the whole deal, especially since we had a full roster one day and the next day, we didn't have a team."

"Sam, what did you do?" Jude asked. Sam took his time before answering.

"I pleaded my case with the club president, but he said it was a done deal. I asked how they made the decision about who would be the head coach. The president told me that I didn't have enough experience to be the head coach. I blew my top. I informed this jackass that I was the only one of the coaches that had actually played soccer and that I had coached longer than any of them."

"Didn't the parents complain?"

"Of course, they did, but the club told them that they either played on the assigned teams or the club would refund their money. I told the parents to let the boys play. I hoped to sort the mess out later."

"You should have seen what went on when we showed up for our first practice. Sam knew the coaches from playing against them, but he didn't really know them. The head coach was a school teacher named Coben. Rick Coben had never played soccer or any sports from the look of him. Coben's assistant coach was a little German guy named Franz. Coben gathered everyone around him before making introductions. We all had to say our names and tell a little about our soccer background. After all the introductions, Coben introduced Franz, but never said a word about Sam. Sam was a little put off by the slight, so he loudly cleared his throat and announced that he was Sam and he was also one of the coaches."

"I take it this Coben guy wasn't happy having Sam as one of his coaches."

"Jude, that would be an understatement. The first practice went downhill from there."

"Mac, what did the guys that played for dad think about what was happening?" Marie had come back into the room joining the conversation.

"Most of the guys didn't want to play for Mr. Coben because they had either had him as a teacher or knew someone that had had him in school. Coben wasn't well liked among the guys, but your dad did a good job of selling the merger by pointing out how much better the team would be with the best of both teams playing together."

"That makes sense, but I can't imagine dad being happy with the situation. What about that, dad?"

"You know that I wasn't happy. I was pissed-off. The move was about politics. They wanted to have select recreational teams. This wasn't about not having enough players. We had enough until the club removed some players from our roster and told a couple others that they were too late to sign up. The people running the club knew this teacher, but I had never gone to any club meetings or spent my time brown-nosing the board members."

"What happened when practice started?"

"Franz and Coben explained that the most important thing the team needed to do was learn the pre-game warm up routine. The team spent over thirty minutes doing this stupid drill over and over again. I have never seen any team do anything remotely like this drill. After this excruciating ordeal, we finally started soccer drills, but this turned into a strange shadow drill that was done for another thirty minutes. The drill involved a lot of dribbling and defenders just following the dribblers. Mac would take the ball from the dribbler and get yelled at by Franz. Poor Mac ran a lot of laps during this drill. With just fifteen minutes left in practice, Coben put the guys in positions. Every one of my guys were now defenders. It didn't matter where a kid had played before, if they came from my team, they were defenders. When the offense came towards the goal the Bootleggers all shadowed the play right into the net. I asked a player why he didn't take the ball or at least try and stop the offense from scoring. He looked at me and said, "We're not supposed to.""

"You didn't go ballistic, dad?"

"Marie, you have to remember this was the first time both teams had worked together. I thought that these were just kinks that would work out as we went along, but the worst thing was that Franz yelled so much that he made the boys cry. Franz didn't know squat about soccer, Coben knew even less. Most of the boys had been playing for them from the time they started, so they thought this was the norm."

"Marie that wasn't the worst of it, there was another coach that came out occasionally; Mr. Beard."

"Mac, what was wrong with Mr. Beard?"

"Mr. Beard was also a teacher, but at a different school. Beard only showed up for games at first. The problem with that was that he expected the guys to play differently in the games compared to what they were being taught at practice during the week. Beard would be yelling one thing, Franz would just be yelling, and Coben would run up and down the sideline screaming, "Dibble, dribble, dribble.""

"What did the players do, Mac?"

"I remember just trying to block out all the stupid yelling and screaming, but I got pulled from one of the first games for not doing what Franz was yelling, even though his accent was so strong that no one knew what he was saying most of the time. I was so upset that I felt like I couldn't breathe by the time that I reached the sideline. Sam came over and tried to calm me down. Franz got in my face and told me I wasn't going to play anymore. Coben asked Sam if he would explain what Franz wanted me to do. Beard apologized for yelling by claiming he was just trying to get my attention. I went back into the game, but we lost badly that day."

"At this point, I was receiving phone calls from irate parents. These wonderful coaches didn't play the kids as much as the rules called for. Plus, adding the yelling imbeciles to the mix, all this added up to was upset kids, parents, and one coach. I made sure that I was early for the next practice. Most of the time I'm in the middle of the players as they warm up. I walk around, kick a few balls, and talk or tease the guys. The other coaches always stood off the field talking. That day I didn't go onto the field. I approached the other coaches and told them that we needed to talk. I declared that the yelling and screaming at players had to stop. I, also, informed them that the rules called for every player to play at least half the game. Parents were complaining and that I would back them up with the club on this issue. Franz was furious. He claimed that I knew nothing about coaching, further he stated that my kids must not want to win or compete. I almost lost it. I was mad about waiting to confront Franz over the way he treated Mac in the game and now he was putting me and the boys down because they stood up to his bad behavior. I moved towards that little piece of shit and let him have it with both barrels. It took a few moments to restore order. Coben and Beard, both admitted that their wives had complained about the yelling, too!"

"Did things change after this?"

"I wouldn't say that much changed, except the team began winning. The yelling and screaming slowed down as we went on a winning streak, but Franz made at least one or two boys cry at every practice. I took a more active role coaching the kids at practices. My players trusted me to smooth things over on the field. The holdover Bootleggers, slowly, started to see that I would calmly explain situations and show them what they needed to do on the field."

"How did you end up coaching your own team again?" Marie knew well enough to know that I wouldn't stay with abusive coaches for very long. I have told coaches to knock it off when they are starting to lose it during games. I've confronted parents that are yelling negative things at players, too!

"Well, the season was winding down and it seemed that things had calmed down. All we had left was the qualifying tourney. This is when the shit hit the fan. I didn't realize that the three maniacs put all their eggs in the qualifying tourney. There was a two-week break from last league game to the tourney. Coben, Franz, and Beard turned into raving lunatics as the team worked out for the tourney. The volume went up, the crying intensified, and punishments were heaped on any player that ran afoul of them. Franz and Beard came up with new formations and changed positions for most of the players. While all this was going on, they were announcing that at the tourney they didn't have to play everyone."

"That's amazing. These kids got them to this tourney, but they were changing everything and not going to play the kids. Dad, didn't you do anything?"

"Sadly, I didn't do enough. I was receiving phone calls after every practice. Parents were upset about the treatment that their boys were getting from these coaches. At this point, I told them to call the club and that I'd back them up. I remember talking to an old teammate about this and telling him that I was going to talk to the club, but that I knew that I was going to end up the odd man out. My buddy told me that getting rid of these guys would almost be worth getting heaved out."

"Sam, what happened at the tourney?"

"We went down in flames. Changing formations, playing styles, and positions was too much to do with young teenagers. They also didn't play a few of the boys in the first game, so when we headed for the second game, we only had eleven players. Parents took their kids home and bombarded the club with angry phone calls. Franz and Coben got cautioned for their sideline antics. The referee warned them and finally came over and let them have it. The ref didn't card them but reported them to the state officials."

"So, they gave you your team back."

"Not quite, Jude, the club couldn't ignore the amount of complaints and the spectacle at the qualifying tourney. I called and talked to the club. It seems that this wasn't the first-time complaints had rolled in about Franz. The club removed Franz from coaching. They named Rick Coben and I as co-coaches. The club president called me at home and told me that I would be the official head coach, but he wanted me to make sure that Coben was treated as an equal. I was so happy to have Franz gone that I agreed to the conditions. What I didn't see coming was the train wreck Coben would become."

"What do you mean by that?"

"Just that the second season coaching with Coben was even more miserable. It seems that the club president didn't want to ruffle anyone's feathers, so he told Coben that he was the head coach."

"So, the club set you both up for a fall."

"That's how it worked out. Right from the beginning, Rick tried to make all the decisions. We didn't argue or fight in front of the kids, but everything was strained. I won most of the disagreements. Coben spent a lot of time early in the season lamenting the loss of Franz. I didn't say much about Franz except that I felt that Franz caused his own downfall because of not playing the kids enough and his outburst at the qualifier. The thing that kept the coaching issue from boiling over was that the team was winning. What triggered the final blowup came in the middle of the season. Coben went on vacation and missed a week's worth of practices and a game."

"He took vacation in the middle of the season. That's hard to believe. Shoot, dad, you've never missed a game or a practice in all the years that you've coached me." Marie had a bewildered look on her face.

"I don't know that I've missed more than a handful of times since I started coaching. The week was great. I ran practice and didn't feel second guessed with every move that I made. The players told me that they loved soccer when I ran practices. Coben's son didn't go with his dad. That boy relaxed and seemed to be having fun as we worked out. The weird part was that Beard showed up and watched practice from the parking lot. Later, I found out that Coben asked Beard to keep tabs on me."

"This story is insane. Didn't they care about the boys and the team?"

"Marie even my teammates that had played for the Bootleggers before the merger told us that the coaches sometimes were even worse than what we had seen. The players liked Sam a lot, but their parents wanted Coben. It was a real crappy time for all of the players. Guys quit that could have been decent players. It wasn't much fun with Franz and Coben."

"Mac, what was that kid's name that Coben told his mom that I was picking on him?"

"Tad Shipley. You were trying to show him how to play outside back. Everybody felt really bad about him quitting."

"Tad Shipley, that's my new history teacher." everyone turned and looked at Joey as he made his announcement.

"I wonder if it's the same guy."

"Yeah, dad, we had to stand up and introduce ourselves in class. After I said my name, he asked if I was related to the Simone's from Auburn. He told the class that he used to play soccer for a Sam Simone. I told him that was my dad."

"It's a small world. I can't remember if he ever played again."

"I played against him in high school and college. The first time that I saw him playing after he quit the team was in high school. He looked like a different guy on the field. He was a tough little player." Mac added.

"That makes me feel better about what happened. I can't recall any other player that I coached leaving like he did. This kid was a smart, nice, guy that I'm positive had never failed at anything. Straight A student that was involved in the community; just a pleasure to have on the team. But the problem was that he wasn't playing a position that suited his skills. When I first watched him play, he was sadly lacking in the fundamentals to play defense. It was painful to watch him get beat time after time for easy goals. Tad started losing his confidence. The game wasn't fun for him anymore. Tad went from being the first kid at practice to one that came late and even skipped practice. I talked to Coben about switching Tad with Travis or another midfielder, but all I got was Coben's standard answer, "That's where they've always played.""

"What did you do, dad?"

"I started working with him on positioning and staying home. Every time that I saw Tad leave where he should have been exposing his area to a quick pass and score, I stopped practice. Tad always had a reason why he had left his area, but I pointed out how fast a good team would find his place empty and exploit it."

"I've seen you do that a million times, why was this different?"

"Because this kid had never been the one to be singled out for doing something wrong. Tad didn't know how to handle it. If I had moved him to midfield his being out of position wouldn't have left us so exposed. Maybe I should have pushed the issue, but I didn't. Tad's mom talked to Coben the professional school teacher. Coben's dislike for me sealed Tad's fate with the team. As soon as Tad was gone, I revamped the lineup, the defense gave up over two less goals a game from that point."

"Okay, Sam, how did this end up? We don't have all night." Jude knew that I could get a little long winded.

"We were headed for the end of the regular season which meant the qualifying tourney would follow. Coben and his cohort Beard wanted to play to win in the qualifier. Their idea of playing to win was to only play the best eleven. I had handled the substitutions all season. Every ten minutes players were subbed into the game. Everyone played over half the game. It didn't matter to me what the score was subs went in when it was their time. This irked Beard, he started making noise about the tourney about a couple of weeks before we were to play. I guess that I didn't give him the answers he wanted, so after our last game there was a big confrontation in the parking lot. Needless to say, it wasn't pretty. Most of the team witnessed this ugly exchange. I was told to eff-off a few dozen times by these so-called pillars of the town."

"What happened after that?"

"Those two chuckle-heads called the club and expressed their fear of coaching with me. The sad part was that I didn't curse at them or make physical threats. The club called and talked to me about the problems. We finished the season. I thought that it had been resolved, but just as we were gearing up for the next year; I got a phone call from a board member that I'd never met wanting to talk to me about what happened last season. This man informed me that he had to make a decision whether I would be allowed to coach this year. He didn't like my answers. This person expected that I would make nice and be willing to coach with Coben under another head coach, but I fooled him, I gave him my real feelings about the last two years and Rick Coben. My response knocked the club official for a loop. I was not going to be allowed to coach the team. I told him it was their loss and the boys, too!"

"The club sent you packing and kept this Coben guy, wow! So how did you get back into coaching?"

"Mac still wanted to play, so I talked with his mom and dad about him playing in Auburn. When Mac told his teammates what he was going to do most of them followed him. There were enough guys signing up to play that Auburn let them form a new team with me as the coach. The Auburn club didn't have any problems with me because I had played for the club and the high school."

"One club kicks you out and the other club greets you with open arms. Did you play against your old team and Coben?" Marie wanted to know.

"We played them twice a year for the next three seasons and we never lost to them."

"All of us guys that had played for the Bootleggers would really get up for the games with our old team. We wanted revenge on that jerk Coben. During the games Coben would be on the sideline losing his mind as we took his team apart. Sam wouldn't show any emotion as we kicked butt. After the game when we shook hands with the Bootleggers sometimes Coben wouldn't come out and shake Sam's hand."

"Dad, why didn't you get into this Coben guy's face and give it to him?" Marie always wanted action when she felt wronged by someone.

"I wanted to, but it would have made me just like Coben. I had a team with most of my players, so I just did my job the way that I always had. More of my kids went on and played high school and beyond. You know that my measure of success is how many kids that keep playing and learning the game."

"And winning comes with learning. Winning is last on my list of goals. Be the best player you can be and winning will take care of itself." Marie knows all my pet sayings. This started a contest between Mac and Marie to see which one could remember the most Sam-ism's as they liked to call them. The two of them were laughing and yelling out their versions of my sayings as fast as they could. It was pretty amazing to hear the number of ones that came out, but also how many of these sayings weren't even ones that I had ever said.

"Are you comedians done yet?"

"Oh, don't be such spoilsport, dad. You know how we feel about you as a coach. Geez, you know that I haven't liked any other coach that I've ever had because they never measure up to you. We may laugh and tease you about your sayings and intensity, but I wouldn't have it any other way. I bet Mac feels the same way." I knew how both felt. Mac was coaching now to pay back the chance he got when I coached him. Mac may never have played because both of his parents worked, so they couldn't make it to a lot of after school activities. When I started coaching, I figured that Mac and his buddies would be a good place to start. Mac became a good player because he got a chance. There have been many players that blossomed because a coach gave them a chance.

"I know that. It just hit me that, so many players fell through the cracks when all this crap was going on. Tad Shipley was one of about ten or so players that left the team because of the way they were treated by Coben and Beard. I haven't thought about getting fired and those lost players for a long time."

"Sam, you couldn't save all of them, honey." Jude knew that every one of those kids even the ones that I couldn't remember still bugged me.

"I really do know that, but it still irks me that the club would choose an abusive, bad coach over the kids."

"Hey, I have to get going; early day tomorrow. Practice is Thursday? First game on Saturday is at ten."

"That's right. See you on Thursday." Mac made his exit. After Mac left Jude and I made sure that David was ready for bed. I read him a couple of his favorite stories before he nodded off for the night.

"Do you want to watch the news?"

"Sure, Jude, I'll be there in a minute." I stopped in my office/den and started scanning the wall. I had pictures of all the teams that I'd coached on the wall. I'm pretty sure that most of the teams are on the wall. For some reason I felt drawn to look at the photos of those teams. The talk of my being fired from my volunteer coaching position still tears at my guts. The faces of the boys from my first teams smile back at me with all their youthful swagger and charm. Most of these kids are now grownup and raising families of their own. When I reach the team photos of the Bootleggers, I remember some of the incidents that shaped that time and led to my being fired for siding with the boys against Coben and Beard. Bile seemed to bubble up in my mind as I relived those miserable seasons. I felt as impotent now as I did then. The thought that I failed these boys still haunts me.

"Sam, you can't change the past. I know how much you put into coaching every child that plays for you, but I know and believe that most of your players, past and present, do know how much that you cared for them. Come into the living room and sit with me. Don't let these ghosts haunt you." Jude reached out her hand and I took it and followed her into the living room.

PART TWO

MAC INVESTIGATES

Mac pulled into the yard parking lot about an hour earlier then he normally arrived. He knew that his desk would be piled high with paper work from the crossing accident. Mac needed to get a start on the report if he was to make it to practice after work. The yard office was transitioning from night shift to day-shift. Mac grabbed a pop out of the vending machine and started to unlock his office door.

"Mac, I'm glad you're here. Last night a switch crew discovered an open boxcar. It appears to be a robbery."

"Do we know what was stolen, Joe?"

"I don't know what was stolen, but the shipping papers confirm that six containers are missing. The stuff was going to Green Valley Technologies in Kent. I have all of the contact information in the report."

"Thanks Joe, I'll follow up with a contact with the company. Anything else hot right now?"

"No, but I did file most of the statements from the crossing accident."

"Great, I'll finish up the rest and you can get out of here if you want to."

"I think I will. I can hear my pillow calling me from home. It's been a long couple of days." Joe didn't take but a couple of minutes to log out and head for the door.

Mac turned on his computer and started looking through the reports on both the theft and crossing accident. The crossing accident was soon completed and filed. It would now be up to the local police to find the owner of the car. The crew had passed their drug tests and the downloads had shown that the crew hadn't violated any rules leading up to the accident. The results relieved Mac because he hated to take guys out of service when they were just doing their jobs. Railroads had become a lot like Big Brother with all the new technology: cameras, recording devices, drug tests, etc.

Mac grabbed his phone calling the yardmaster. "Auburn Yard how can I help you?"

"Hey Dickie, It's Mac Delac do you have a minute?"

"Sure Mac, what's up?"

"The shipment that was broken into last night can you give me a little background on how long it was in the yard and how often this company gets shipments."

"Let me pull it up on my screen. That car was there for three days. The company gets three or four loads every two or three weeks. They only receive loads on Thursdays. The Valley local handles these loads. The empties are collected when they call us."

"Do you recall any problems with their loads before?"

"Nope, if we had you would have gotten a call or an alert."

"That's what I thought. Thanks Dickie.?"

Something was gnawing at Mac about the theft. Mac decided to do a little research into Green Valley Technology before talking to them. A computer search produced quite a few articles about the company. The company did a lot of government work. It seems that Green Valley Technology and another local firm Puget Sound Industries were locked in a tight bidding war for a new contract with the Department of Defense. None of the articles gave much information on what the technology was, but the winner would be set for years and the loser might go under. This information just increased Mac's growing suspicion. Mac left a message for the day shift agent and headed out to his car. Mac merged his patrol car onto SR167 heading northbound. The freeway was crowded. Kent and Auburn are only about six miles apart but driving the Valley Freeway made it seem much further.

Taking the Willis Street exit, Mac turned towards the West Valley Highway. The large warehouse of Green Valley Technology was only a few blocks north of Meeker Street. It was a newer building. Mac had never noticed it before. The Valley had changed a lot during the last few decades. The farms were for the most part gone, replaced by asphalt, and large warehouses. Progress wouldn't be denied.

Mac walked into the spacious lobby. A kiosk in the center of the room was manned by a security type. A man in a dark suit and an earpiece looked up as Mac pulled out his badge and identification.

"How can I help you, Special Agent Delac?" The dark suit was very friendly and professional.

"I'd like to speak with your General Manager or an assets manager about a shipment."

"Let me see if I can find the person or persons that you should be talking to. Please, have a seat and I'll call you." The security guy pointed Mac towards a waiting area. Mac found an empty chair and sat down. The lobby was very busy while Mac waited for someone to appear. Just as Mac began to doze a man walked up.

"Are you Special Agent Delac?"

"Yes, I am."

"Please follow me."

Mac followed the man into the corridor behind the security kiosk. Nothing was said while the two men walked down the long hall. The man finally stopped, opening a door while ushering Mac in. Mac looked around the large office. The man backed out of the office leaving Mac in silence. The walls were covered in photos of military and political functions. There was a door on the left side of the room. Furnishings were tasteful, but expensive looking. Mac was admiring some of the artwork on the shelves behind the desk when the door opened. A tall man dressed in a dark blue suit that like a glove walked in extending his hand to Mac.

"Sorry to have kept you waiting, but I was in a meeting. I'm Paul Layton." Mac shook the well-manicured hand. Paul Layton had the firmest grip Mac had ever felt.

"Mac Delac, Special Agent in Charge, Cascade and Pacific Railroad."

"How can I help you today?"

"Yesterday or the day before a shipment heading to Green Valley Technology was broken into at the Auburn yard and six containers were stolen. I have the numbers of the containers that were stolen."

"Good, we can see what was taken and work on replacing the items. Do you have any leads on the culprits?"

"No, but I believe that there was more than one involved. An abandoned car was left on a crossing. The timing of the accident and the thefts, are too coincidental in my opinion."

"My staff or I will be glad to give your department any help that you need."

"I understand that your company and Puget Sound Industries are competing for a very lucrative government contract. Do you suppose that the thefts have anything to do with that?"

"I couldn't be sure until I check to see what was stolen, we have many customers. If I find anything that I think is beneficial to your case, I'll call you. It's been nice meeting you, but I'm late for a meeting. My assistant will show you out." Layton picked up some folders and quietly left the room. His assistant graciously led Mac out.

"This is Layton, they've taken the bait. I just had a visit from the railroad police about a theft from one of our shipments. The numbers match the targeted items. If everything plays out, we should be leaving Puget Sound Industries in the dust. Yes, I've already set the cleanup in motion." The call ended.

SAM'S IN A FUNK

I was just finishing the daily banking when Linda walked into my office. Linda pulled up a chair and sat down. Linda is one of my closest friends and the manager of the Auburn Good Samaritan Store. We had worked together for over decade. Recently the Society had made some changes on the board. I became the Executive Director of Stores and I promoted Linda to store manager. It might be one of the best moves that I've ever made.

"Is everything okay, Bossman?"

"Yes, for the most part. Last night Joey told us he had a new teacher. Turns out to be one of my old players. This started a discussion about an incident that happened when I was coaching Mac and this teacher. I haven't talked about what happened for years."

"What happened?"

"I got fired from coaching for standing up for my players. I had been coaching Mac's team for about five years when the soccer club decided to merge my team with the club's other team in our age bracket. It seemed that this club would decide which team gave them a better chance to win district and state titles. Mac's team wasn't chosen to be the anointed team, so we were forced to merge with a team called the Bootleggers. The club informed me only a couple of weeks before the start of the season. The kids had no choice as to where they could play.

Rosters and teams were set. I was told that I could be an assistant coach on the new team."

"What did you do?"

"I pleaded my case for the kids and our team, but my words fell on deaf ears. The only way for the kids to play was for us to go along with the club's decision. This unholy alliance lasted two years. At the end of the two years, I was once again the head coach. The other coaches had never played soccer and knew little or nothing about the game. The main problems were that the other coaches were considered movers and shakers in the club. The last season there was a big, ugly, blowup in front of the players and their parents. The sad thing was that I wasn't the one dropping F-Bombs and making threats, but I was the one that got fired. I haven't talked about this to many people over the years, but Joey mentioning his new teacher brought on a discussion of the teacher and the time period."

"That was a long time ago, most parents would pay extra to have you coach their kids. I've watched you work with your teams over the years. You really care about those kids."

"I know all of this, but I still fret about it."

"Bossman, every time an old or current player of yours comes in and calls you "Coach" your eyes light up making your day."

"You're right, as always, but I get back as much as I give with those kids."

"That reminds me of the other reason that I came in here. Some woman came in right after we opened and she's the spitting image of your ex-wife."

"God, I hope it's just a look alike. I don't need any more trips down memory lane." Linda left my office. It must be over seven years since I've talked to my ex. I guess that I'll do my morning stroll around the store. If it is Jane, I'll just try to be cordial.

The store was busy for this time of the morning. I headed towards the furniture department. The area was overflowing with merchandise. I'll need to talk to Linda about having a sale. The appliance area was pretty empty, so I headed for the book corner. That's when I spotted her. Jane hasn't changed much in appearance since we parted, but there was something different in her carriage. Jane had always been up or on. Boisterous, loud, the center of attention, even unwanted attention. Jane craved attention. Today, her body language was subdued. I walked towards my ex. This was the woman that I once loved with every inch of my body and soul. The demons that she was always chasing or fleeing from hadn't completely killed my feelings for her, but her leaving made my heart hurt. Plus, she harmed Marie and Joey more than she had hurt me. That's what put the nail in the coffin. I was able to keep my shit together only because of the kids. They needed a stable parent to help them heal. My wounds slowly closed, but never completely healed.

"May I help you?" Jane turned at my question and there was a look of surprise in her eyes.

"Sam, I wasn't sure if you'd be here, so I've been browsing around trying to get my courage up to ask someone if you were here." There was an awkwardness as we stood just two feet apart. Jane and our history make up so much of who I am; both the good and the bad. Part of me wanted to reach out and hug her, another part of me wanted to scream at her.

"It has been a long time. What made you come here today?" I was leery about Jane's appearance.

"Well, it's kind of complicated. Things aren't going very well in my life, in fact, they haven't been for a long time. Don't say anything, I know that I created most, if not all of my problems, but as I've been trying to sort out all of my crap it dawned on me that the only time in my life that I ever had anyone on my side, either to listen to or help me with my problems was when we were together."

"If I remember it right, you never listened to a word I said. In fact, you told me that you were a grown woman and that you didn't need or want my stupid advice."

"Don't get mad. Yes, I said and did all of that and more, but almost everything that you told me has turned out to have been right. I destroyed our marriage and family from the inside. Not once since we split, have I ever felt the feelings that you gave me. I ran from what I was looking for. I don't know why I came here today, but I had an overwhelming need to talk to you today."

"I'm still angry about what happened, but I have made a new life with a woman that I love. The family is as healed as it can be after all we went through. We've spent these years working to rebuild our world."

"I don't know what I wanted coming here. I can't fix the chasm that I created with the kids. I just knew that for my sanity, that I needed to see and talk to you. I'll get out of here. I don't want the board to jump you about me being in the store." Jane started to leave. Something made her change her mind and she turned around and hugged me. The hug startled me, but the tears streaming down her face disturbed me even more.

"Sam, are going to be okay?" Linda was standing next to me. I wasn't sure how long I'd been there.

"I don't know. That woman has always been able to completely throw me for a loop."

"What did she want?"

"That's just it, I don't have any idea. She said that things haven't been going well for her. She came to see me because I was the only one in her life that had ever listened or been there for her. I reminded her that she had never taken my advice, in fact, telling me that she didn't need or want my advice."

"You better be careful; she's got something up her sleeve."

"I'll be careful, she won't get a chance to hurt me or the kids again."

"Sam, can I ask you a favor?"

"Sure, why not?"

"Can you work the till for about a half hour? I need to finish some training with my store employees."

"The till might be just what I need to wash this funk off of me." Linda and I walked towards the front counter.

"Angie, Sam is going to cover the store while we go finish the training."

Linda and the store employees headed to the break room for the training session. If I needed any help, I would call for Bob's group from the sorting room. An elderly woman gingerly approached the counter.

"Young man, can you tell me which color tags are on sale? I don't see very well without my glasses."

"Blue are fifty percent off, green are twenty five percent off, plus you get a ten percent senior discount."

"Thank you very much. I always seem to forget my glasses at home." I started picking up around the counter when the phone interrupted my busy work.

"Good Samaritan Store, how can I help you?"

"Do you take donations at the store?"

"Yes, we do. What type of donations do you have?"

"Mostly just clothes and household stuff. How late are you open?"

"We accept donations until six. Make sure that the donations are bagged or boxed. If you want a receipt, ask when you get here."

"You say that donations are accepted until six. I think that we can make it. Thank you." The line went dead. I spent the next forty minutes ringing up sales and answering the phone. It's always been good for me to work the counter. It helps me to keep a pulse on what the employees face, also what the store might need.

I spotted Angie working her way towards the front counter. Angie stopped every few feet to help or talk to a customer. Good customer service is very important in the second-hand business. We face competition from other chains, swap meets, and garage sales. Angie has shown me that she's a very good with the public. She gets her work done and is helpful with the customers.

"Let me finish with this sale before I hand the till over to you."

"Take your time, you look like you're enjoying the work."

"I have to agree with you. It has been enjoyable, especially after my encounter with my ex-wife."

"That was your ex! I don't know if I could have talked to my ex-boyfriend and not been completely out of whack."

"Let's just say that I'm partially out of whack." We both chuckled at my bad joke.

I felt a need to retreat to my office. The encounter with Jane seems to have thrown me harder than I first thought. It was too early for lunch, but maybe I could catch Jude in a free moment at work. The phone was ringing as I waited for Jude to answer. Jude was the one person in my life that keeps me from turning into an overbearing ogre.

"Jude Simone, how can I help you?"

"Do you have a couple minutes?"

"Sure, it's kind of slow, what's wrong?"

"You're not going to believe who was just in the store looking for me."

"After all these years, what did she want?"

"God, you know me well. That's part of the problem she didn't seem to know why she came. It appears that Jane's new life didn't turn out any better than her old life."

"Well, okay, you've always known that was probably the case, so why come to see you now?"

"I don't know. Jane mentioned that I had been the only one in her life that ever listened to her and cared."

"That might be true, but she must have had a reason to want to see you."

"She never got around to any reason, especially after I pointed out that she disregarded any advice that I had ever given her, she also use to tell me she didn't need me to tell her how to live. The reunion ended shortly after that. When she left, I started thinking about all the crap that she had put me and the kids through, plus add that to the stuff that we talked about last night has made me want to rip a door off its hinges. Outside of my dad's death those are the things that make me white-hot angry when I think about them."

"Let's see if we can relieve some of that anger. I wouldn't want you going around ripping doors off their hinges. Can you get away for lunch in about an hour?"

"Yes. Where do you want to go?"

"I'll meet you at home. Lunch is on me."

"Thank you, honey."

The Good Wife

I set the phone down and calmed down a little. How uncomplicated life could have been if I'd met Jude earlier in my life. Jude is my rock. I know that I'm strong, but Jude has helped me regain the strength that I lost dealing with Jane's emotional turmoil that left me and the kids wounded. The hour moved at glacial speed. I was not only out of whack, but maybe I'd lost my whack completely. I couldn't stand it anymore, so with a tremendous effort I went looking for Linda to tell her that I was leaving.

"Get out of here, Bossman, go get some therapy from Jude."

"I don't know how long that I'll be gone."

"Bob and I can handle it. Go and try to relax."

I didn't need someone to smack me in the head with a stick. I was in my car and heading home in a flash.

Jude's car was in the driveway as I turned on our street. Just seeing her car made me feel better about the start to my day. I thought that I was past the agony of my first marriage, but every bad thought and emotion came rushing back over me as I talked to Jane. Seeing Jane stirred up stuff that I should have shaken by now. Jude is the only person that I can talk to about these feelings. This is not what I want to talk to my wife about, but she has the touch when I get all balled up and out of whack. Thinking these thoughts has already started the process to calm me down.

I stepped out of my T-Bird looking around my yard before heading into our house. The house was very quiet. Quiet as a tomb. The quiet forced me to move slowly towards our room. The door opened exposing an empty room. There is a light on in the master bath. Gently, I push the door open seeing my beautiful wife soaking in the garden tub. She's under a mountain of bubbles. A wine bottle and two glasses are on the counter.

"Come on in the water is fine."

I start throwing my clothes off. Soon, joining her in the tub. The water was fine. The water starts to throw off the anguish of the morning as I snuggle with my wonderful wife.

"This is just wonderful. I wouldn't have thought of a bubble bath in a million years." I said as I hugged Jude. I've hit the mother lode. We sipped some wine. Letting our love soak through us. We made slow, lazy, love before we had to go back to work.

There was a new man driving my T-Bird back to work. This man felt on top of the world. The love I feel for Jude is indescribable. My vocabulary isn't large enough to put into words all that she means to me. I wish that I could never think of Jane again, but I know that I haven't purged all that junk out of my system.

LITTLE OLD LADIES AND NEW HUSBANDS

"Mrs. Dantone it's so nice to see you. Can I help you with your stuff?"

"Thank you, Sam, please, take my keys and open the trunk." Mrs. Dantone handed me her keys and I opened the trunk of her ancient Mercury. She handed me her bags as I loaded the car.

"How is your family?"

"About the same as always. I only see the kids and grandkids when they want something, but that's better than most of my friends. They hardly ever see their kids. How's that lovely wife of yours?"

"Well, she's the most beautiful woman in the world."

"I remember when my husband Vince used to say that about me. I sure miss the old goat." Mrs. Dantone was smiling and tearing up at the same time. She did this every time she mentioned her husband Vince. He'd been dead for over ten years. They used to come into the store together shopping, laughing and talking. As a boy, I used to see them at Sunday Mass. Vince would make the rounds at the coffee hour and entertain all the parishioners with wild stories and jokes. I hope that someone smiles and cries over me when I'm gone. Mrs. Dantone joined the Good Samaritan Society after Vince died. She is one of the most active members. The Dantone smile was a welcome sight for most of the people that the Society helped. If all our volunteers were as nice and helpful as Mrs. Dantone, everyone would be in a better place.

"You have a wonderful day, Sam. Thanks for helping me with my bags. I've got some families to visit." Mrs. Dantone waved as she started her car before she pulled out of the parking lot.

"You look like a different man. Jude is a miracle worker."

"I don't know about a miracle worker, but she's a keeper." Linda laughed at my comment.

"It was pretty quiet while you were gone, but there are a few messages on your desk."

"I'll check them out right now. Would you have Bob come to my office? By the way we need to have a furniture sale. The area is overflowing with merchandise."

"I was going to talk to you about that before your visitor showed up. Let me know what type of sale you'd like, and I'll make it happen."

"After I talk to Bob, we'll work something out."

My office was a little stuffy when I walked in. The place looked the same, but there was a large pile of messages sitting squarely on my desk. Just the sheer number of messages politely waiting for me to answer started to change my mood. I slipped into my chair and picked up the first message. It was from Jane. Tension washed over my body. I reached for the next message. Jane again. This went on for most of the messages. Only two messages weren't from my ex-wife. No contact for almost a decade. But, today a visit, ten messages all in one day. I must have done something bad in a previous life to be rewarded with this much aggravation in one swoop. A knock brought me back from my nightmare.

"Come in!" I shouted.

"Is it a bad time, Sam?" Bob looked as if he was heading to the gallows.

"I'm sorry, Bob, I wasn't yelling at you. Come in and take a seat."

Bob sat down. I needed a moment to compose myself. Bob was nervously glancing around the room. He looked like he was searching for an escape route. I know that I have the reputation for scaring employees on occasion, but Bob has never had my wrath aimed at him. After mentally giving myself a pep talk, I felt ready to talk to Bob about the reason that I called him to my office.

"Bob, trust me everything is alright. The reason that I wanted to talk to you is that the trucks need to be set up for servicing. They need to be taken on different days. Before they go, the drivers need to fill out the check-list for any problems that need to be fixed. I want to see the check-lists before the trucks go in for service. While I have you here, is there any other equipment or building maintenance issues that need addressing?"

"The bailer needs to be looked at. It seems to be hanging up when we use it, also, there is a leak over the back of the break room."

"Okay, I'll call the service rep from the bailer company. Would you talk to Floyd's Construction to come out to look at the roof?"

"Sure, Sam, I'll call them right away. I'll let you know about the trucks." Bob looked like a man given a last second reprieve as he scurried out the door.

I turned back to the messages that seemed to be mocking me from my desk. "Angela, would you come into my office, please?" I didn't wait for a reply. Angela was in my doorway in a flash.

"You wanted me, Sam?"

"Yes, I have a question about these messages. I presume that you took the messages."

"Oh yeah, all of them. What would you like to know?"

"I'm not sure, but did she say anything about what she wanted?"

"No, not really, but she sounded disturbed."

"Disturbed, how? What did she say?"

"She didn't say much any of the times she called, it was more of how she sounded. It seemed as if she was distracted. I can't put my finger on exactly what her problem was, just that she kind of spooked me."

"That sounds like I felt this morning when she was here. She gave me the impression that something was wrong, but not what it was. Thanks, Angela, I just wanted a little more information before I call her back." Angela left the office. I hesitated before summoning up the courage to return Jane's calls. Tensely, I listened to the phone ring. Just when I thought it would go to voice mail someone answered.

"Who is this?"

"Sam, I'm returning Jane's calls." It wasn't Jane. A man's voice had answered.

"She ain't here. Don't think that I don't know about you and Jane. I won't put up with this crap like her ex-husband did. What a smuck."

"Well, whoever you are let's get a few things straight. First off there is nothing going on between Jane and me, secondly, I am her smuck of an ex-husband. Jane left ten messages at my work today. It made me think that she was having some type of emergency."

"Okay, so maybe you're not the one she is messing with, but why did she call you after all these years."

"That's is exactly why I called. I wanted to see why Jane had contacted me after all these years. By the way, what is your name? I don't believe we were ever formally introduced."

"Rod Jones, I know that we've never met, but I've listened to years of Sam Simone stories from Jane. It always made me wonder why she left you and those kids. The "Great Sam Simone" has been a huge shadow over our marriage. Jane started acting stranger than usual about three or four weeks ago. At first, I didn't think anything about it because she goes through lots of phases, but I guess that I don't need to tell you that. A couple of weeks ago, things took a turn for the worse."

"Well, Rod, I never was told anything about you or why she left. I've spent the time trying to help the kids heal and fixing myself. Today, was the first time that I've heard from Jane since the divorce was final. This sudden contact with Jane has thrown me for a loop. If you see Jane tell her that I returned her calls. I need to get back to work."

"I'll tell you this Sam, if Jane contacted you at work, there is something serious going on." The call ended on that note.

ANGRY COACH

There was a note on the counter when I walked into the kitchen. Jude had gone shopping with David. Joey was out with friends and there were sandwiches for me in the fridge. I grabbed a sandwich and a soda. Marie came in already in her workout clothes.

"Good you're home. We have to pick up Suzy on the way to practice."

"Would she die if she walked the three blocks to the field?" I snapped harder than I wanted.

"She might. You are in a crabby mood today. What's wrong, Dad?"

"I'll tell you about it later. While I get ready would you lock the doors."

"Sure!" Marie went off to check doors and I finished my snack before heading off to get ready for practice.

We pulled up in front of Suzy's house in Twin Rivers and Marie jumped out to get Suzy. Fred, Suzy's dad, walked over to the car. "Hey Sam, another season starting already. How do you think the girls will do this year?"

"They should do all right. The tournament this weekend will go a long way to answering that question. Are you going to be out there cheering the girls on?"

"I was planning on it if the mountain doesn't blow." Fred almost always answered any question with if the mountain doesn't blow. The girls came bounding out of the house. We headed towards the soccer park.

Mac and about half the team were already on the field warming up. Marie and Suzy helped unload gear from the car. More players showed up as Mac and I set up the field for some drills.

"How's it going today, Sam?" Mac asked as we set up cones.

"Very strange day. I had a visit from Jane."

"You're ex-wife, Jane?"

"The one and only. I wasn't in a very good mood after talking about Coben last night, so when Jane appeared at the store my day went downhill from there."

"Was it just a social call or did she have a reason for coming by?"

"If she had a reason for showing up, she never got around to telling me before she abruptly decided to leave. As she was leaving, she did the damnest thing, Jane turned around and gave me a hug."

"Whoa, Jane gave you a hug. I remember, during the time of the divorce, she would have rather had a car run over her than to touch you."

"My brain has been in turmoil all day. If I act up at all during practice, please just excuse me and accept my apology in advance."

"Is this a retroactive apology for all the times that I've seen you act up during practices?"

"Very funny, but I wouldn't quit your day job. Call them in for practice."

Mac told the players to put the balls on the line and to make a circle. After all the balls were on the line and the girls were in a circle, Sam stepped into the circle and began to go over some instructions for the tournament. While he spoke, the team was stretching.

"I see that everyone is here. That's good because I don't want to repeat everything that I've said a second time. At the end of practice, make sure that you get a tournament schedule and packet."

Sam and Mac were handing out practice vests to start the workout when a commotion broke out among a few of the girls. "Is there a problem?"

"No coach, no problem at all." Wendy Smith answered for the girls involved in the commotion. Most of the time Sam would let the offending party or parties settle down and go on with practice, but to the amazement of the team, Sam went ballistic.

"Get on the line, everyone! Since the team isn't ready to practice, maybe conditioning is what the team is ready for. Five burners at full speed. Go!" Burners are full field sprints up and back five times. A lot of teams don't do much running, but as a coach I've always been an advocate of the philosophy that the team in the best shape will have an edge on the field. The team finished the running and lined up waiting for what was coming next.

"Take a break and then get into your groups again." The rest of practice went along the same way. A goof-up resulted in more running. At the end of practice, the team hadn't been sent to the line for at least twenty minutes. The girls looked very good during the scrimmage. They were moving and passing with precision. Mac gave the signal to gather up the gear and come together by the goal. Mac did most of the talking at the end of practice.

"Remember, pick up a tournament packet before you leave. You guys looked sharp out here tonight. That's what we need to see out of you during the tournament. Everybody, help haul the gear to the car."

"Marie, what's up with Coach today?"

"He seemed really mad at the world."

"I'm still tired from all the running he made us do." It seemed like every player asked Marie what was wrong with her dad.

"I'm just as baffled as you guys, he came home from work and seemed mad. I asked what was wrong and he told me we'd talk about it later. I don't like Burners any more than you guys." The girls all laughed. It seemed to break some of the tension.

Mac and Sam were talking by Mac's car. "Sam, relax, you'll find out why she came by and it will probably be nothing. I must say that this practice may be in the top-five most, laps at practice, that I've ever seen."

"Once, it got away from me, it just kept going, but they looked good at the end of practice. Aggressive passing and movement from the offense and the defense didn't back down at all. I'll see you on Saturday."

"Dad, Suzy says that she's not sure if you're going to give her a ride home or make her run."

"Lost my mind a little out there, okay, I get it. I need to mellow out. I'll see what I can do."

"Sam, we looked good out there today, didn't we?"

"Yes, Suzy, you guys looked great out there. I'll try to tone it down. I'm not sure what got into me."

"We love you anyway, coach."

MAC AND QUEENIE

Mac got out of his car and headed towards the entrance. The door opened, and a couple danced out lost in the moment. Mac chuckled, half with envy, but mostly out of the knowledge that he hadn't danced out the door with an attractive woman in a long time. The room was overflowed with people relaxing after a hard day at work. Music filled the room. The band was playing some almost forgotten hit as the crowd listened, drank, and danced the night away. Mac made his way to an open spot at the bar.

"Mac it's been such a long time since you've graced us with your presence! What will you have? It's on me." Jody smiled as she greeted Mac.

"A schooner of Rainier, please."

"Come over, sit at my table." Jody pointed to her regular table and Mac followed Jody and his beer.

After they were settled, Mac took a long swig of his beer. "God, I needed that. I just spent the weirdest soccer practice with Sam that I can remember. I've seen some weird practices with my cousin, but tonight takes the cake."

"What happened?"

"When we first got to practice it seemed like Sam was all out of sorts. He told me that if he acted strange to just accept his apology in advance. He proceeded to make the team run Burners every time someone screwed up. This went on the whole practice. I asked him what was wrong. All that he would say was that Jane showed up at his work today and gave him a hug."

"His ex-wife came to his work, why?"

"That's the problem she didn't or couldn't tell him what was up, just that she needed to talk to him. This came on top of him telling the story of getting fired from coaching."

"Sam got fired from coaching, when?"

"It happened when he was coaching me. I'm not sure how it was brought up, but Jude and the kids wanted to know what had happened, so Sam told them."

"I never knew about that. So, what you're saying is that last night a very private thing came out and today the woman that broke his heart showed up and wanted to talk, but gave him a hug instead. Wow, you know Sam as well as anyone, he's like a brother to you, his reaction seems consistent with the Sam I know. These are two of his biggest failures or regrets. It's a wonder that he just made the girls run. Sam can be a bear when he's out of sorts. I'm sure he'll be okay in a few days."

"I wish that I could be as certain as you are, but I guess that you're right."

"I am. So, Mac, how's the love life?"

"Dead. As dead as it's ever been, why?"

"I know someone that is just perfect for you. She's young, pretty, and she has a job."

"Jody, do you remember the last time?"

"How was I supposed to know that she had walked away from Western State?"

"You have a point. Has Tim met her?"

"As a matter of fact, he has. He has given her his rock star seal of approval."

"What's the rock star seal of approval?"

"Tim having been a rock star for such a long time developed a crazy meter when it comes to women. Tim placed her at the lowest end of the crazy meter." Jody waved at her staff to bring another round for them.

"Thanks for the beer and conversation. I have to be going after I finish this one." Mac finished his beer, gave Jody a hug and kiss before heading out the door.

SAM'S ANNOUNCEMENT

"Thanks for the ride, Sam. See you tomorrow Marie." Suzy sprinted into her house.

"Dad, what's wrong?"

Sam took a moment before answering Marie's question. "I had a visit this morning at work."

"Who came to see you?"

"Your mother showed up right after we opened."

"Jude's my mother, that woman is just the person that gave birth to me." The two rode along in silence for a few minutes. "What did she want after all this time? Did she ask about Joey and me?"

"I don't know what she wanted. I'm not sure that she knew why she was there. The only thing that she said was that she needed to talk to me. And no, she didn't ask about you guys, but she wasn't there long enough to say much."

"Did you have a fight with her?"

"No, nothing like that, just that she wanted to talk to me, but before she said anything, she told me that she was leaving. As she left, she stopped, came back, and gave me a hug." Marie was quietly crying as I told her about her mother's visit. I reached over and hugged my daughter as tears streamed down my face. The rest of the drive home was spent in silence with each of us replaying the heartbreak that was my ex-wife and Marie's ex-mother.

"Dinner is ready get cleaned up and sit down." Jude was loading the table up with Chinese food. The smells coming from the takeout food quickly changed Sam's mind about not being hungry. The family came from different directions taking their usual places around the table. As soon as everybody was seated, food was dished up at a frantic pace.

"How was practice?" Jude asked between mouthfuls of Mongolian Beef.

"Dad was in epic form. He made us run more Burners in one night than we usually do in a season."

"God, I wish that I'd been there to see that." Joey chuckled at the thought of Marie running all those Burners.

"Honey, is everything okay? I know that you like to condition the team, but this doesn't sound like regular conditioning."

"I don't know. This has been a day that's made me feel like biting people's heads off. Nothing that I've done helps."

"Daddy, I love you."

"David, thank you, I love you, too!" Sam reached over and gave David a squeeze. Sam's boiling anger started to recede with him being surrounded by his family.

"Sam, I thought, that after lunch you seemed better about seeing Jane. What happened?"

"When I got back to work there were nearly a dozen phone messages from Jane, but when I called her back her husband answered. I think he told me his name is Rod. It seems that Rod doesn't know where his wife is or why she would come to see me."

"You're saying mom came to your work and disappeared."

"That's the gist of it, Joey."

"She didn't even ask about us Joey."

"Does that surprise you? She hasn't tried to contact us for years. It's not as if we meant anything to her all this time." Joey's voice was full of sadness and anger. Joey as rule never said much about Jane. He kept his feelings bottled up. Once not too long after Jane left, Joey asked me if his mom left because we didn't love her enough. My heart broke again as I told him that none of this was his or his sister's fault.

"I don't know what's going on with her, so for now we'll just have to wait and see why Jane chose to contact me." The rest of the meal was finished in silence.

Sam woke up early after a night of tossing and turning. Sleep hadn't refreshed him. Sam sat up drenched in sweat.

"Honey, are you okay?" Jude reached out to comfort her husband.

"I honestly don't know. I can't remember what I dreamed about, but I was agitated all night."

"You tossed and turned like you were fighting off demons."

"Maybe I was, Jane has always brought out deep emotions whenever I've seen her. I thought the anger was gone, but I may just have been fooling myself."

"Are you sure that she didn't give you an idea of why she had to see you?"

"No, I became defensive as she started telling me that I was the only one that ever listened to her. All my memories, good, and bad, came flooding back as she was talking. I was already on edge after talking about soccer the night before. Most of the time I pride myself on being able to keep myself together under stress but look at me right now." Jude held Sam for few moments without saying anything.

"Sam. I love you. Get in the shower or you'll be late for work."

David was sitting in the bedroom when Sam finished his morning shower. David's face lit up as his dad came into the room. "Daddy, I was waiting for you. Momma says that breakfast is ready. She said to hurry your butt up."

"She did, did she, well we'll have to see about that. come here and give your dad a kiss."

David giggled and ran to Sam leaping into his arms. The happy duo headed towards the kitchen.

"Momma, look what I found. Can I keep him?"

"I don't know, he looks like he needs a lot of care. Do you think that you're up to taking care of an old Italian guy?"

"He's not so old. He smells good, too!"

"Okay, you can keep him for a while."

"No Mom, don't give in so fast. I bet he'll expect to be fed every day. Pretty soon we'll all be waiting on him hand and foot." Joey was laughing as he gave his objections.

"I don't think we have a big enough yard for him. The neighbors will complain when he goes outside in shorts." Maria had to add her two-cents worth to discussion.

"I still want to keep him, please!" David was still in Sam's arms as he said this.

"I'm glad someone wants to keep me. As for you two, you're both out of the will."

"We love you Dad but remember that we'll be the ones that decide which home you go into when the time comes."

"That thought has crossed my mind many times, many times." Everyone laughed as we all sat down for breakfast.

JANE CALLS BACK

Sam left the house with a lighter load than the one he woke up with. The T-bird started up first time, the radio rocked some Burton Cummings as Sam pulled out into the street. The commute wasn't long enough to mull over much. The last couple of days weighed heavy on Sam's mind. When Sam lived in Twin Rivers, he could plan out a good part of his day on the half-hour ride to work, but once he moved back to Auburn it took maybe ten minutes to get to the store leaving little time for work planning or daydreaming. The T-bird glided into Sam's designated parking spot with a good fifteen minutes to spare. Living so close had made it easier to make it to work early, letting Sam get a jump on the day.

"Hey Bossman, remember today is the manager's meeting. Is ten, okay with you?" Linda greeted Sam as he walked into the store.

"Sure, is everyone going to make it?"

"No cancellations so far."

"Ten this morning in the employees meeting room, thanks, Linda."

Sam opened his office door. The room was small and very spartan. The white walls were covered in graphs and notes. The only personal items in the room besides his family pictures was a small refrigerator that sat in the corner filled with diet cola. Sam used to have to stop for his diet sodas at the convenience store next to the bank that Good Sam's had an account with, but when a small dorm room type refrigerator came into the store; Sam bought it. The appliance repair guys checked it out to make sure it was working. Sam grabbed a can of soda out of the frig, sitting down to go over his notes and papers for the manager's meeting.

As Sam was finishing his preparation for the meeting, Angela opened the door. "Sam, you're wanted on line one."

"Thanks, Angela." Sam reached for the phone. "Sam Simone, how can I help you?"

"Sam don't hang up. I'm sorry that I left before I could finish talking to you."

"Jane what do you want?" Sam was trying to be as calm as he could, but it was hard not to let Jane have it for showing up and tipping his hard-fought composure on end.

"I'm in trouble. I got myself mixed up with a really, really, bad man. He's made threats and I don't want to be around to see if he's going to carry them out."

"Why aren't you talking to your husband, Rod?"

"I can't talk to Rod. Rod has never trusted me enough to listen to much of what I say. Our marriage isn't a very intimate one. Most of that is my fault, but if anyone knows what it's like to be married to me it would be you."

"Listen, I don't know what you want from me, but the days of me being willing to do anything for you are long past. Tell me what you need. I'll see if there's anything that I can do. You need to call your husband and at least tell him you're okay."

"I met this guy named Rick. We hit it off and one thing led to another. I won't go into all the sordid details, but the affair was starting to fizzle out when I found out that Rick was into some shady things, so when I tried to break it off with him, he told me that he would let me know how and when we would be over."

"Okay, he didn't want to break up. Stop taking his calls and eventually he'll back off."

"No, Sam, you don't get it he made threats to hurt Rod and the kids."

"You and Rod have kids?"

"No, Marie and Joey. I don't know how he found out about the kids, but he had your address and enough information about the kids to scare the crap out of me."

"For crying out loud, you show up in my life after all these years and all the damage that you did to us with a story about some guy that's nuts and is making threats towards our children. Children that you haven't had contact with in nearly a decade. How the Hell am I supposed to help you fix this?"

"Sam, I've watched you solve problems for years. In the last year or so, you've cleared up murders and ended a hostage situation. I don't know how or what you do, but this is for the kids and me. I know that you don't owe me anything, but I remember how much you loved me before I killed your love."

Jane was sobbing as she stopped talking. Sam had no response for Jane's request. After a few moments of quiet sobbing Jane had one last request, "Please, Sam."

"All right, Jane, I'll see what I can do. I'll need a little more information about this Rick and a way to reach you."

"I don't have much about him. The information is on the way as we speak. I won't give out my number. I'll call you at work."

"You must have been pretty sure that I'd help if the information is on the way."

"I've never seen you not help someone in need. Thank you." The line went dead. Sam's amazement was interrupted by a knock on the door.

THE GOOD SAMARITAN'S COME TO THE RESCUE

"Come in." The door opened as an elderly woman gingerly walked through.

"Are you the manager?"

"Yes I am. My name is Sam. What can I do for you?"

In a halting voice the woman started to speak. "I don't know what to do. My husband is very ill, and I've had to spend almost all our pension check on trips to the hospital. I don't drive, but I need to be with Joe as the doctors try to find out what's wrong with him. The bus doesn't run by our apartment, so I have to call for a taxi to get me back and forth to the hospital." The woman seemed to wind down as she spoke.

"Do you have any family in the area?"

"No, they all live in Spokane."

"What's your name, ma'am?"

"Oh gosh, I didn't introduce myself, I'm Henry. That's short for Henrietta."

"Let me take you to see Julie in our Society office. We'll see what can be done to help you out." Sam reached out his hand to guide Henry to Julie's office. Sam gently led her across the store and found her a seat outside the office. "Let me have a word with Julie before you come In."

Julie waved Sam into her office. "What do you have for me?"

"That's Henry. Henry's husband is sick. Henry has been running up a big bill getting back and forth to the hospital. I was thinking that this might be a good time to enlist the help of Charley and Josephine to help her with transportation and maybe even a place to stay when her husband needs her. Tell them that I'm calling in all my markers."

"I bet that you won't have to call all your markers in. Charley loves to help when I call. And you know that Josephine has never let us down." Julie was smiling as Sam went out to bring Henry in. Sam knew that Henry would be in good hands as he headed back to his office.

"You short changed me! All of you morons try to steal from the customers." A large intoxicated looking man was yelling at Angela.

"Sir, I gave you exactly the right change. I counted it back to you."

"Well you counted it wrong and if you don't give me my change I'm going to."

"You're going to do what? I don't think that a tub of lard like you is going to do anything. I would bet that if you're not out of this store in the next minute you'll find out what I'm going to do to you."

"You can't talk to me that way. Let me talk to the manager. You won't have a job when I'm done."

Sam stood for a moment before addressing Angela, "Go ahead and call the manager."

"Sam, would you give me a hand with this customer?"

"Angela, what seems to be the problem?" As Sam spoke the unruly man began to get confused.

"This man paid for his items and now claims that I short changed him."

"Let me see the transaction. Everything seems to be in order. I believe that you owe my employee an apology."

"Why you rotten bastard, I'm going to kick your ass." Sam was in front of the till in a flash. He leaned in real close to the belligerent customer and whispered in his ear.

"If you don't get out of here right now, I'll hurt you like you've never been hurt before. If I ever see you in this store again, I'll make you wish that you'd never been born." The menace in Sam's voice and deadly stare he gave the man was enough to make the drunken fool nearly piss his pants.

"I guess that she gave me the correct change. I'll take my stuff and leave." The man walked out. He began running across the parking lot. The store released a collective sigh as the situation ended.

"Thank you, Sam. Are you okay?" Angela was looking at Sam as if he had grown a third eye. She was spooked by the amount of anger that had boiled out of Sam during the confrontation.

"What? Oh yeah, I'm fine just a little tense. I hate these confrontations, but it didn't look or sound like that guy was going to listen to reason."

"What did you say to him? He left like his pants were on fire."

"I'm not sure why he left in such a hurry. I quietly pointed out what was going to happen if he kept up his rude behavior." Sam's intense look and body language slowly started receding. The air in the store was choked with Sam's intensity. The room was still very quiet. The customers couldn't be sure of what they had just witnessed. To Angela's surprise, Sam went back to his office and came out a moment later with a folder. He appeared to be completely relaxed and calm. "Angela, I'll be in a meeting for about an hour. If an emergency comes up, I'll be in the employee meeting room."

"Okay, Sam, I'll try to handle things for an hour."

"I'm sure that you'll do just fine. You do a good job working with the public." Angela watched Sam head off like he didn't have a care in the world. It was a Jekyll and Hyde moment. Sam had been acting so different since his ex-wife had showed up.

EMPLOYEE MEETING

The employee meeting room was all a-buzz with amazement about the way Sam had handled the drunken, rude customer. Most of the crew had witnessed Sam diffusing these types of encounters before, but this morning's incident was different. Sam usually used a lite approach. He mixed in a little humor and small talk to stop any escalation of the problem, but this morning from all accounts, Sam had been menacing in his contact with the man. The employees that had witnessed the event felt fear when Sam whispered into the man's ear. The color drained from the man's face as Sam leaned over and whispered to him. The fact that when the customer left the store he began sprinting as if someone was chasing him spooked everyone watching the incident.

"Good morning. Anyone that's not part of this meeting needs to get back to work." Sam announced as he walked into the meeting room. Employees not involved with the meeting left very quickly. The supervisors grabbed their notes and beverages and sat down around the meeting table. The meeting room was used as a combination break room/meeting room as needed. The room had several cafeteria styled tables with chairs and the usual microwave ovens and an employee refrigerator. Posters and work-related memos covered the walls. The back of the room had places for the employees to hang their coats and work smocks. The room got a lot of use from the Good Samaritan staff.

"Sam are you okay? Do you want me to start the meeting?"

"I'm fine. It was a little intense for a few moments, but it turned out okay. We'll just run the meeting as usual. I'll go over the charts and the few announcements before turning the meeting over to you. Linda, make sure that you stress that the quality of merchandise needs to be consistent when we send it to Enumclaw and Covington."

"That's my number one priority."

"Well, let's get this sucker on the way." Linda sat down, and Sam took his place at the head of the table. "Attention everyone, before we get started, I know that most, if not all of you, are aware of the little disturbance that just happened in the store. There isn't much to tell. An unruly customer was making threats to Angela when I stepped in and ended the situation. Everyone one of you as supervisors have faced and will face similar situations in your stores. I'm not going to tell you that there's a right or a wrong way to handle these problems, but I don't want anyone getting hurt or worse, so if something escalates call the police and make sure that your staff and the other customers are safe. Any questions?" The group looked at each other without anyone wanting to be the one to ask Sam what he had said to the man.

"I don't think so, Sam, go ahead and start the meeting." Linda smiled at Sam as she nervously tapped the table.

"Yeah, let's get started. Linda would you hand out the store statements to everyone?" Sam gave Linda the statements. Each of the managers started looking over the papers as they received their copies of the statements. Sam chuckled as he watched each manager checking to see the progress of their part of the pie. The group worked hard. Each one cared about how their hard work contributed to the overall stores' performance. The better the stores did, added to the Society's ability to help the needy. Today's statement, Sam knew would bring smiles to all the managers. The changes made by the Board had improved the stores in most areas.

"As you can see the stores are doing quite well. Every one of you have met your goals. You all deserve praise and thanks. The Society is very pleased with the way the stores have been growing. There's nothing official, yet, but in a few days, each of you will be getting a small bump in pay. Before I turn the meeting over to Linda, I still need the reports from all managers about their stores needs and issues. I can't go to the board and request new equipment and repairs without these lists. On a sad note, Father Eugene will be leaving Blessed Family. I know that I'm going to miss him. I don't know who'll replace him as pastor or on the board. So, with no further ado, Linda will handle the rest of the meeting." As Linda moved toward the head of the table, Sam gathered his notes and departed. There was a moment of shock as Sam gathered his things and departed. Sam never left these meetings. Linda was surprised, but she didn't blink an eye as she took over the meeting.

"Linda, what's going on with Sam? He's been different for the last couple of days. Almost weird even for him."

"I'm not sure, but his ex-wife came to see him a couple of days ago. She has always been able to knock him for a loop, but beyond that I don't know for sure what's bugging him."

"Linda, can we go over these store reports?"

"Yes, I'll try to walk everyone through them."

Sam opened his office door. Not one customer or employee had stopped to talk to him as he made his way back from the manager's meeting. Most of the time, Sam would be approached multiple times if he was wandering around the store. The incident before the meeting seemed to be keeping the public at arm's length. Sam chuckled to himself thinking that he might want to steer clear of him, too, after his display.

"What ya chuckling about?" A shrill voice pierced the silence.

"Josephine, what brings you out in the daylight?" Josephine Barrels was standing behind Sam cackling and grinning. Josephine was ninety plus years old, making her the oldest ex-employee Good Sam's was likely to ever have. Josie was barely five feet tall on her best day, but she had always stood ten-feet tall in Sam's eyes. Sam considered her family. She was one of the few people that could bust his chops and make him smile.

"What the hell do you think brought me out in the middle of the day? I'll tell you. It's these disturbing reports about all of this crazy behavior, Sam."

"What crazy behavior?"

"Don't act all innocent with me, Sam Simone, I've had people calling me for the last few days telling me about all of your crazy antics. Not thirty minutes ago, Rosa Dantone called and told me about the man that went running and screaming down the street. So, what gives?"

"Come into my office and I'll try to explain, by the way, who brought you today?"

"Jody brought me. She takes me grocery shopping every week."

"Jody's here?"

"I'm right over here, Sam." Jody moved towards the office. Sam and Jody hadn't seen much of each other since Jody and Tim got married. Sam turned and faced Jody. Jody looked fabulous. Marriage sure seemed to agree with her.

"Wow! You look great. Tim must be doing something right." Sam gave Jody a hug.

"Don't squeeze her to death." Josephine cackled.

"Come in and sit down. Two of my favorite women in the whole world have come to spank poor Sam for misbehaving."

"I wouldn't say that, but we are concerned about your wellbeing. The reports about this week don't sound like the Sam we know and love."

"So, what gives with all of this hostility?"

"I guess to answer both of you is I'm not sure what has set me off. I was okay until the other night when a subject came up that I have rarely discussed with anyone. I was kind of churned up about this discussion when Jane showed up at work the next morning. I seem to have been on a tear ever since."

"That worthless ex-wife came to the store. Why?"

"Josie, that's the problem, she couldn't tell me why she came. When she finally gave an answer, it had nothing to do with me or the kids. Just that she is in some kind of trouble. She wants me to help her."

"Did you throw her out? No of course not. She knows you well enough to know that you'd help her out if she was in trouble."

"What are you going to do?" Jody quietly asked.

"I'm doing some checking into the man that she's having problems with, but I don't see what, if anything that I can do to help."

"Once a cheater always a cheater. I tried to warn you about her all those years ago, but you were in love. Even I couldn't get through your thick head when you're in love." Josie didn't cackle this time.

"Yes, I loved her, but that isn't the problem this time. It seems that she is in way over her head and either the husband is involved or he won't help her. I guess that I'll help, but every angry thought and feeling that I've ever had about her seems to have pushed their way to the front. I just can't get past my anger."

"Maybe, if you let your friends and family help, you could release some of the anger. You've spent a long time holding all that garbage in. Let it go."

"Jody, I wish that all of this would just go away, but seeing Jane again just stirred everything up again. Let's not talk about my crap. How are you guys doing?"

"Just fine, Sam, Tim is playing a few shows back east, but I couldn't take the time off to tag along and be his groupie."

"I offered to go in her place. You should have seen the look of terror in Tim's face. I laughed so hard I almost peed my pants."

"We didn't just stop by to talk about your crazy behavior, Julie called and asked Josie about helping some woman with a sick husband."

"You're talking about Henry. She came into my office and I felt that the best way to help her was with rides to and from the hospital and maybe a place to stay if things got bad for her husband."

"We're going to pick her up at the hospital and get to know her over lunch at Josie's. In fact, we need to get moving to make it there on time." Josie and Jody gave Sam hugs.

"Jody, there's something very different about you. You're radiant. Tell Tim I said good job."

"Sam, you are a ninny. Jody hasn't made a public announcement, yet, but she's..."

"Oh My God! Really?" Sam grabbed Jody and hugged her with a flood of happiness and joy. This news seemed to crack the anger that had been encrusted around Sam. Tim and Jody are having a baby. Tears were streaming down Jody's face as Sam hugged her. The emotional scene was interrupted by Josephine's voice.

"Sam, let her down, we have to go meet Henry."

"Okay, you guys have a good day and take care of Henry."

SAM STARTS TO FIGHT BACK

Sam sat quietly thinking about the emotional roller coaster the last few days had been. Ex-wife, babies, old friends, and people in need had turned his life inside out. Finally, Sam knew what to do. He picked up his phone and dialed a number.

"Hey, Sam, what do you need?"

"Hey, Fatty, I need you to do some research. Background checks on a couple of people. Do you have a moment to take down some information?"

"Yeah, sure, let me get a pen. Is this for the store?"

"No, it's for me. I'm doing a favor for a friend."

"Okay, give me the information." Sam gave Fatty all the names and things he wanted. Fatty quietly took all the information before asking Sam a question. "How soon do you need this? Isn't Jane your ex-wife?"

"A couple of days should be fast enough. And yes, Jane is my ex-wife. Fatty make sure you bring me a bill for your services."

"Our regular rates for this; it shouldn't be too much work."

"That's great. Oh, Fatty, don't let anyone know what you're doing. I don't know for sure what Jane has got herself into."

"Not to worry, I don't leave tracks or talk in my sleep." With that Fatty ended the call.

Jody and Josephine pulled up in front of the Hospital. The women didn't know what Henry looked like, but they figured that they'd find her without too much trouble. Jody wasn't driving her big Dodge today because Josephine usually had a large amount of groceries to haul home, so Jody was driving her Ford Escape. The two friends started towards the entrance when Jody spied an older woman sitting just inside the door looking kind of lost.

"This way, Josie." Jody pointed towards the woman inside the lobby.

"Excuse me, ma'am, is your name Henry?" Josie smiled as she asked the woman.

"Yes, I'm Henry." There was a hesitation in the woman's answer. She checked Josie and Jody over pretty well but was still unsure what they wanted.

"I'm Josephine and this is Jody. You talked to some people at Good Sam's this morning and we've come to see if we can help you while your husband is in the hospital."

"Yes, I talked to a very nice man and he tried to help me. The lady in the office said that someone would come by and pick me up and maybe help me. Are you the ones they sent?"

"We sure are. Let's get in the car and we'll go over to Josie's house for lunch and try and work out how we can help you. Let me take your arm and we'll go to my car." Jody helped Henry up and the three women went out to the car. There wasn't a lot of talk as they rode to Josie's house, but when they pulled into the driveway, Henry seemed to have relaxed a bit. The three women unloaded the car and went into Josie's kitchen.

"Just put those bags down on the counter. I'll put it all away later. Grab a chair and I'll make us some coffee."

"I don't mind helping while you make the coffee. Henry, sit down and make yourself comfy."

"I'd like to help, too! Just tell me where everything goes. If all of us pitch in, we'll have more time to sit and talk." Soon all three women were busy putting groceries away and making coffee and snacks. Josie's kitchen wasn't very big, but it gave off a feeling of home as the new friends hustled about. Josie had lived in her house for nearly fifty years. Josie and her husband had bought the little house after their kids had grown up. The years went by quickly. Josie's kids now had grown up children. Josie had been a widow for over twenty years, but not a day went by without her thinking of her husband and kids. The house was the one constant in Josie's life. The kitchen was always the heart and soul of the house.

"Don't be shy. Dig in and try some of the cookies and sandwiches. How do you like your coffee, Henry?"

"Just a little cream and sweetener, thanks." Jody set the creamer out for Henry. The ladies were busy for a few minutes eating sandwiches and cookies while drinking the fresh roasted coffee. When it seemed that everyone had their fill Josie reached for her phone.

"Excuse me, I need to see if Charley is home." Josie dialed the number. "Charley, do you have your pants on? That's good.

Can you come over to my house? Great, see you in a few minutes." Josie placed the phone down on the counter.

"Who is Charley?"

"Charley is an old friend. He is going to help with transportation when your husband is in the hospital. I figure that we can work out the details when Charley gets here."

"Don't worry, Henry, Charley used to run the Good Samaritan store. Josie worked for Charley and Sam, Sam's the man that helped you today. All of this was Sam's idea. Sam tries to help anyone in need. If Sam can help, he'll find a way."

"Sam sounds like a good guy. How long have you known him?"

"I've known Sam since high school and Josie's known him since he was five or six years old."

"Well, I wish that I'd met him or known about him a few weeks ago, it sure would have been a load off my mind."

"Henry, you're not the first person to say that." All the women smiled and laughed at that thought. The doorbell rang. Charley had arrived.

PART 3

THE TOURNAMENT

The final bell of the day sounded at Twin Rivers High School. The students started filing out of Mr. Shipley's Contemporary American History class. "Joey, could I have a word with you? It won't take long."

"Sure, Mr. Shipley, what do you need?"

"I understand that your dad coaches your sister's soccer team and that they have a tournament this weekend. I'd like to watch them play and say hi to your dad, so I was wondering what time they're playing and where."

"The games are going to be in Alpac at some new complex there. I think the first game is at ten on Saturday. I'll double check tonight and bring the information to class, okay?"

"That would be great. Thanks, Joey."

"See you tomorrow." Joey sprinted out of the classroom to find Ginger.

Tad Shipley turned around and opened his desk drawer. He pulled his cell phone out and pushed a button. "Hey, it's me, I just talked to Sam's son, Joey, he's going to bring me the schedule tomorrow. The games start Saturday morning. I'll let you know about times and pick you up on Saturday."

"How are you today, Mrs. Rosalini?"

"Pretty good, Sam, I always like it when the boss comes out and takes care of me." Mrs. Rosalini smiled and blushed like a school girl.

"I like to give special service to my favorite customers. I don't see Mrs. Blevins. Is she not feeling well today?"

"Oh, I thought you knew, Sally had to go into assisted living about a month ago. She was having a rough time keeping up with everything, so her family decided to put her in a home. I offered to let her come stay with me, but the kids thought that wasn't a good idea because Sally and I are so close in age. I try to go see her every other day. Sam, she isn't doing very well in there." Mrs. Rosalini had tears running down her face.

"You two have been friends forever. I'm so sorry. When you have a moment give me her room number and I'll see about going to see her."

"We've been best friends for nearly seventy years. I don't know what will happen if I lose her." Sam stepped around the checkout stand hugging Mrs. Rosalini while she cried. Some of the people in the store had seen the incident with the abusive man that Sam had run off, but now they were witnessing a completely different side of him. Sam Simone was a complex, yet simple man, that was at his best when he was helping someone in distress. Sam grabbed Mrs. Rosalini's purchases and slowly guided her to her car.

As Sam came back into the store, Linda wrapped her arms around Sam and kissed him on the cheek.

"What was that for?"

"That's for being my hero. That may have been the nicest thing you've done in a long time. Mrs. Rosalini is one of our oldest customers and you did exactly the right thing to comfort her."

"Stop it, I'll have tears in my eyes if you don't stop gushing about such a simple human gesture."

"No, it wasn't a simple human gesture otherwise everyone would do it. No one else stepped up to the plate. Sam, don't ever change."

"Are we ready to close?"

"As soon as the last customer is checked out. We will be."
The phone rang as Sam and Linda were talking. "Let it go, Sam.
If it's important they'll call back."

"No, I'll grab it while you guys finish closing." Sam stepped
into his office and picked up the phone. "Good Samaritan's. How
can I help you?"

"I always loved your voice. I wasn't sure if you'd still be at the
store." Jane's voice cut a cold path through Sam's body.

"Jane, what can I do for you?"

"I was wondering if you've found out anything since our
conversation the other day."

"Nothing yet, but I have someone checking a few things out.
I'm expecting him to give me the results tonight or tomorrow. It
would be easier to handle things if I had a way of talking to you."

"No, that's not going to work. I'm using pre-paid phones to
talk to you and my husband. When you get some more
information, you will see my reasons for all of this. I'll try and
call you tomorrow." The connection ended. Sam didn't put the
phone down for a few moments. Sam's anger and resentment
towards Jane rose into his throat causing him to feel ill.

"Sam, are you okay?"

"No, I don't think so. That was Jane."

"What did she say?"

"Nothing. She wanted to know what I'd found out about her
problem, but she wouldn't or couldn't tell me where she is or how

to get a hold of her. When she hung up, I felt my insides churning. I feel like a pot that overflowed. It seems that Jane can still bring out the worst in me."

"Go home and relax with your family." Linda put her arm around him, giving him a hug.

"I can't go yet, I've a phone call to make. It's better that I make it here."

"Would you like me to stay?"

"Thanks, Linda, but I need to make this call and write some notes about all of this. I promise that I'll go home as soon as I'm done. I'll set the alarm when I leave. Go on, get home to your family."

As soon as the last employee left the store, Sam sat down and called Fatty. Fatty answered right away. "Hey Sam, I've been expecting your call."

"That sounds as if you've uncovered something interesting."

"Scary interesting. This Rick guy is into a lot of things, all borderline illegal, but no police records that I could find. The kind of scary interesting part is this Rick guy and Jane's husband have a long history together. The two have been involved in many schemes dating back to their teen years. The last few months both men have been under investigation by the Attorney General's fraud division."

"Does it say why?"

"No, that part of the records was sealed. So far, I haven't been able to crack it open."

"Keep trying, I think I need to talk to Chief Petty and see if he can give me any insight. Thanks, Fatty, have a good night. I'll talk to you again in a few days." Sam started a notebook about Jane's problem. The fact that Jane was in hiding made Sam feel as if Jane was involved in something more than just a case of an angry boyfriend. He had always known that Jane didn't have a moral compass, so her cheating with a close friend of her husband was no surprise. Sam put the notes into his secure filing cabinet and finished locking up before heading home.

"Dad's home, get ready for dinner." Jude was finishing setting the table as Sam walked in the door.

"Sorry, I'm a little late. I had to make a couple of phone calls." Sam planted his tired body down at the counter. The day hadn't been physically exhausting, but he felt like he'd gone ten rounds with the heavyweight champ.

"You're just in time, it seems that everyone was running a little late today. You look like you had a rough day."

"I feel like I was rode hard and put away wet, between the unruly customers and a crazy ex-wife it was a bad day."

"You heard from Jane again?"

"Yes, right at closing time. It seems that she has worked her way into a mess. I still don't know why she's in hiding, but Fatty has come up with some information and is working on getting me some answers."

"I understand why you're helping her, but what about the rest of the stuff that's been going on. It's not like you to be so Jekyll and Hydish."

"Linda called you about the incident this morning?"

"Actually, Linda and Jody, both called me."

"I can't give you an answer about what happened. When I came out and found this man threatening Angela something inside me snapped and in an instant, I was as angry as I can remember, but the anger was controlled. It seemed to be focused on this jerk. I'm not exactly sure what I told him, but he ran out of the store like his hair was on fire. It must have been powerful because most of the customers and employees all backed away."

"Linda told me that later in the day you held an older customer that was crying."

"You remember Mrs. Rosalini, well it seems that Mrs. Blevins, her best friend, has been put into a home because she can't take care of herself anymore. Mrs. Blevins and Mrs. Rosalini have been best friends for over seventy years. Mrs. Rosalini just lost it when she began talking about her friend. I reacted to her sorrow holding her while she cried." Jude put down the dish she was holding, wrapping her arms around Sam.

"I love you, Sam Simone, don't you ever change."

The next couple of days went by without any blowups, but the crew at Good Sam's left him alone for the most part. Sam was aware of the standoffish behavior of the people around him. The knowledge did little to defuse Sam's tenseness, in fact he felt as if the wider berth everyone gave him only added to the tension. Sam tried to shake off the malaise by getting out in the store helping where ever he was needed, but any relief was short-lived. As Friday crawled to a close, Sam began to get excited about the soccer tournament. Both, he and the kids loved playing in tourneys. If the team did well it would be a great way to start the season. Even the good thoughts about the tournament were fleeting.

"Sam, line one is for you." Linda announced as she poked her head through Sam's office door.

"I got it, thanks, Linda." Sam reached for the phone, "Sam Simone, how can I help you?"

"Sam, it's your favorite ex-wife." Jane's voice knocked Sam for a loop.

"Jane, I'm still looking into the situation, is there something new?"

"No, I've come to the conclusion, that I miss talking to you."

"Isn't it enough that you're having an affair with one of your husband's oldest friends, but somehow in the middle of all this you miss talking to me, your ex, whom I remind you, you haven't talked to in over ten years?"

"Oh Sam, you are still a shit when it comes to me. I know that I messed up our marriage and might be a crappy mom to our kids, but I did love you at one time and I have always regretted putting you through all that misery. I'm in some serious shit, but I'm smart enough to know that you are my best chance of getting out of this in one piece. When all of this is over, I'll leave you alone, I promise."

"Like I said, I'm looking into the information that you gave me, but what I can't see is what your husband and this Coben are up to. By the way, I used to know a guy named Rick Coben. He was a school teacher."

"Yeah, that's Rick. He mentioned that he had coached with you a few years ago. I don't think that he has fond memories of you."

"I wouldn't think he would. I'm not too fond of him, either. What I don't understand is how this school teacher could be involved in so much illegal crap and still be a teacher."

"Rick says that he has always been good at covering his tracks, but that is exactly why he's angry at me. Everything is getting hotter for him and Rod. Rod is also very suspicious about me, because I haven't always been faithful. I know you've already figured that part out, but I won't apologize for not being faithful. It's just not in my genes."

"If you could give me an idea about what Rick and Rod are up to it could point me in the right direction."

"That's the problem, I don't know what they're up to. Rick seems to think that I'm aware of his plans. I knew that when things started getting hot for Rick that I had to split before he hurt me."

For some reason Sam believed what Jane was telling him. Sam used to be able to read whether Jane was lying. His instincts about her started to return as they were talking. Rick Coben was the wild card. When Sam and Rick coached together, Sam didn't like anything about the man, but he never imagined that Rick was anything other than a bad coach.

THE GAMES BEGIN

Saturday morning was bright and sunny. Not a cloud in sight. Sam was up early, making sure that everything was ready for the tournament. Marie had her own routine on game days. Marie made sure that her gear was in her bag and that her favorite ball was placed on top of the contents. Marie listened to the same music on game day while she showered and got ready to leave. Jude and David would come in Jude's car and arrive a few moments before kickoff. This way David didn't get tired and bored too soon at the games. Joey had announced that he might catch the first game, but he had a date with Ginger. The house was alive with activity.

"Who wants some toast and cereal?" Sam called out loudly. The answers came flowing in.

"Sure dad, don't make hot cereal, we'll just have some Cheerios."

"Gotcha, pour your own, I'll make toast." Soon the whole family was grabbing bowls and boxes of cereal.

"Mac's here." Marie hollered to be heard above the din.

"I need coffee." Mac said as he entered the room.

"Fresh pot, grab a cup." Jude pointed towards the coffee. Jude loved game day. The whole world seemed more alive when her family was getting ready for a game. Mac soon had a cup of coffee and sat down at the kitchen table with a content look on his face.

"Long week, Mac?" Sam thought his cousin looked relieved sitting at the table.

"Weirder, than long. I'm investigating a theft that happened while everyone's focus was on an accident that now seems very suspicious."

"Why does it seem suspicious?"

"Well, for one thing, the car that was abandoned on the crossing had all the doors locked. I don't remember any other car ever found with the doors locked. I have a feeling that the persons responsible for the car are the same ones that broke into the box car and stole part of the shipment. I just don't have proof, yet."

"I can't guarantee no weirdness today, but we can always hope."

"Dad, we need to get going in a few minutes. I don't think that we have to pick anyone up, Susie said her dad is bringing her."

"We'll be out of here in plenty of time. Finish your cereal. I've already loaded the car. Jude, you have directions to the field. Joey, I hope to see you and maybe your friend, too! David give me a kiss."

"OK, Daddio," David ran around the table and jumped in Sam's lap and hugged and kissed him.

The new soccer complex in Alpac was impressive looking. Sam thought as the car pulled into the parking lot. There were four, full size, lighted fields. The fields were all Field Turf. This would be a great place to play in the wet fall weather in Western Washington. Everyone started grabbing gear and equipment. The main building in the center of the complex had a small crowd gathered in front of it. Sam, Mac, and Marie headed towards the crowd to find out what field would hold their first game.

"You made it. Isn't this the best soccer fields we've ever played on?" Susie and her dad moved up to meet Sam and company.

"It's pretty impressive. Did you see which field we're playing on?"

"Number two, Marie give me some of the gear and we'll pick our side." Marie gave Susie the ball bag and the two friends headed towards Field #2.

Fred, Susie's dad, reached out his hand, "The mountain didn't blow. That's a good sign."

"I suppose your right, Fred," Sam suppressed a chuckle as he shook Fred's hand.

Sam and Mac checked in at the tournament table. "I need your team and coaches name."

"Twin River Roadrunners and Sam Simone." the woman gave Sam a quizzical look.

"Are you the same Sam Simone that used to coach here?"

"Yes, but that was a long time ago."

"My brother played for you, Buddy Johnson."

"I remember Buddy. How's he doing?"

"Buddy died almost ten years ago in a hit and run accident."

"I'm sorry, I didn't know. Buddy used to make the team laugh with his jokes and impressions of the other guys."

"Buddy was always laughing and joking. One thing, he always said was that you were the only coach that he felt let him be himself."

"I don't know if I let him be anything, Buddy was just Buddy. It's nice to meet you Buddy's sister."

"I'm sorry, my name is Patty. Here's your tournament packet. Good luck, Sam."

"Thank you."

Sam and Mac started walking towards the field. More parents and players had shown up and joined them as they headed towards Field #2. Sam was very quiet as the group walked. The news about Buddy seemed to weigh heavy on Sam. Buddy wasn't the best player, but he made up any short comings on the field by being well liked by everyone.

"Mac, do you remember Buddy Johnson?"

"Sure, funniest guy on the team, why?"

"That's his sister at the tournament table. She told me that Buddy was killed in a hit and run accident over ten years ago."

"Wow, I never heard about that. I keep in contact with a lot of the guys from the team. I'm surprised that I never heard about the accident."

"Me, too! Let's get the girls out there and start their warm ups. I'm going to go over the tourney stuff and getting the player cards ready."

"Sure, Sam, ladies gather round."

"Coach, I'm John Ross. I'll need your players cards and the team lined up for the pre-game inspection."

"Nice to meet you, John, I'm Sam Simone. That's my assistant Mac Delac." I pointed at Mac on the field. "Mac, bring them in." The team came towards the sideline as I gave the referee the roster and player cards.

"Line up and when I call your name step forward." The ref went through the list and checked players for jewelry and shin guards. "After I'm through with the other team, I'll call for captains."

"Petty and Susie are the captains today. Get your armbands and wait for the ref. Everyone else help stow the gear. If you need to use the restroom do it now." A small group hustled to the restrooms while the rest packed gear and set up the sideline.

"Dad, have you seen this team before?"

"No, Marie, but from watching them warm up they don't look like they have a lot of speed. If we can get an early lead, we should be able to out run them."

"I'll try to push hard from the start and we might be able to keep them off balance."

"If that doesn't work, we'll think of something."

"Captains!" Petty and Susie made their way to the center of the field. The coin was tossed. Soon, Petty and Susie raced back to our side.

"We won the toss. We kick off and defend the east goal."

"Gather round. Play your game and everything will work out. You guys have been working very hard, so now is the time to cash in on all your hard work. Mac do you have anything to add?"

"Push it hard right from the start. Don't let down." The team put their hands into the circle.

"One, two, three, go Roadrunners." The starters sprinted onto the field.

"Sam, if we can score early, I think that this team will drop back and let us take the game to them."

"Unless, they were dogging it in warm ups, but I don't think that they can keep up with us."

The game started off with the Roadrunners taking the ball into the box and just missing a goal. Marie and Petty kept up the pressure not allowing the opponents to cross the center line. The goal finally came about ten minutes into the half. At half time, the score still stood 1-0, but most of the action had occurred in the opponent's half of the field.

"Nice half, everyone, go get some water or fluids into you. Is anybody hurt? That's good. Gather round. In the second half, I want us to get wider and make a few crosses. Try to draw them out. Once they come out to defend, we should have a few lanes start to open for some runs or quick passes. Mac make the switches in the lineup that we talked about."

"Susie come out to start the half, Brenda play a wing on the right. Susie stay right by Sam and me because we want you to see, what we need you to do, when you go back in."

"Gather in, play hard and keep up the pressure."

The second half was easier. The other team wasn't nearly as game ready as our girls. The Roadrunners scored twice more as Marie dominated on the field. Every player on the roster played over half the game. 3-0 doesn't look like a big blowout on paper, but Sam and Mac watched as the girls controlled every phase of the game. The final whistle was a relief for both teams. The Roadrunners were happy and tired from the effort in the first game. The teams lined up to shake hands and thank the refs. The opposing coach stepped towards Sam and offered his hand.

"Things don't change much, do they?"

"What do you mean coach?"

"When you coached here and in Auburn your teams were always disciplined and in better shape than their opponents. I played for the Bootleggers after you went to Auburn. We never beat you then and we certainly didn't beat you today."

"It was just a first game and your team did some things very well. We had you pinned on your end of the field for most of the match, yet we only came away with three goals. That was a pretty good defense trying to hold up under a lot of pressure. You've got something to build on. We'll see how it goes when league starts in few weeks."

The end of game formalities was soon over. Parents and players gathered stuff from the sideline. "Everybody, head over to the concession stand to find out when we play next."

The happy gang of parents and players pulled up in front of the concession stand. Some parents were giving their kids money for snacks, others were taking the opportunity to use the restrooms. Sam, Mac, and a small group of parents were bringing up the rear. This group included Jack Petty and Fred Barr. Jack and Fred had the longest tenure among the soccer parents.

"Let me check the tourney schedule. Mac could you find the tourney director? I have a couple of questions."

"Sure, Sam, you said her name is Patty?"

"Yeah, Patty Johnson, she's Buddy Johnson's sister." Mac went looking for the tourney director. Sam moved towards the schedule on the wall of the concession stand. Marie joined him as he was writing down the time and field of their next game.

"Hey, dad, we get an hour and a half break. Have you ever heard of the team we're playing?"

"No, but it looks like they won 1-0 this morning. You guys had a pretty good game for a first game."

"Yeah, but even controlling the ball for most of the game we didn't finish very well."

"That's my take on it, too! I don't know how to grade the defense since they had no action at all. I guess this next game will answer our questions about the defense." Sam turned around and started to move back to his team. A man came around the corner and stopped in front of Sam.

"Well, if it isn't the greatest living soccer coach in the world. The guy that knows more than every person out here." The words were said with a nasty sneer by the stranger.

"It's hard to believe that anyone would still let you coach and abuse kids. Don't tell me that you're destroying more players and still talking shit to their parents. I can smell the shit as I'm standing here."

"Screw you Simone. I should have buried you years ago. You've always underestimated me."

"Look, you little shit for brains, you ran like a coward back then and I wouldn't be surprised if the yellow streak is still there." The stranger started towards Sam just as Mac came back around the corner. Mac quickly stepped in between the two angry men. Jack Petty moved the girls and parents from both teams away from the situation.

"Sam, not here, this isn't the time or the place," Mac added.

"Just as I thought, Sam needs protection. What a joke!" The stranger laughed and walked off.

"I'll kill him, so help me, I'll kill that worthless piece of crap." Sam was almost too mad to hold back. The parents and players had never seen Sam out of control. Sam slumped down on a bench still breathing fire over the confrontation.

"Mac, who was that guy?" Marie's voice was almost hysterical.

"That was Coben."

"That's the guy you were talking about the other day. What a jerk."

"Coben comes off as a jerk to just about everyone. I'm surprised to see he's still coaching."

"We've tried to get rid of him, but he has some deep influence with the club. I've hated him for years. Buddy played for him after Sam was forced out. It wasn't a good experience." Patty sounded bitter as she talked about Coben.

"I liked your brother. He was funny and a good teammate. I'm sorry that he passed so long ago. I've always kept in contact with most of my old teammates, but I wonder why no one ever said anything."

"Not many people knew about it because the details were hushed up. As far as I know, it is still an active case. I guess it doesn't matter after all this time; it won't bring Buddy back." The heartache oozed from Patty.

Sam stood up and moved towards Mac and Patty. The team and the parents were still milling around waiting for Sam or Mac to break the silence after the altercation. Sam gestured for the group to gather around.

"First off, I'd like to apologize for that ugly scene. As I'm sure you've surmised that was not a reunion of old friends. Our last meeting was just about as bad as this one. Please, accept my apology for my behavior. If you haven't looked at the schedule our next game is at 1:30 on Field #3. Please be back by one O'clock. If anyone can't make the next game let me know before you leave. Get some lunch or just relax, again you guys played a pretty good game." The group soon dispersed to get some lunch or relax by watching some of the games being played.

"Well, Sam that was almost an all-time epic blowup."

"Very funny, Mac, Coben has always brought out the worst in me."

"Patty told me that we're playing Coben's team this afternoon."

"That's what I wanted to ask her. I thought it was him, but I needed verification. I guess now everyone's got verification."

"Don't let that jerk get under your skin. We'll be fine, just remember, that you've never lost to Coben as a coach."

"I didn't tell you that Jane told me that her and Coben are involved."

"I thought that Jane is married to some guy named Rod."

"She is, but Rod and Coben are friends. It seems that Jane hasn't changed when it comes to cheating."

"Let's grab something from the snack bar and relax by watching some games."

Mac and Sam bought sodas and hot dogs for themselves. Sam also bought for any of the girls that wanted something to snack on. The coaches and about half of the team walked over to a grassy area between the fields to watch the games and relax before their next game.

"Coach, who was that nasty looking guy?" Suzie asked with concern in her voice.

"Suzie, he is just some guy that I coached with a long time ago, let's just say that we didn't have a very good relationship."

"That was a tense few minutes. Is it true that we're playing his team next?"

"Yes, we're playing his team, but remember what I always say, coaches don't kick the ball or make any passes."

"The team does!" All the girls shouted out before Sam could even finish. This brought on a round of laughter and giggles from the team and their parents. The tension seemed to melt away.

"Alright, let's watch some soccer."

The next hour was spent watching some good and some bad soccer. The parents and players that had left to eat or relax elsewhere began trickling in rejoining the group. Sam watched a little soccer, but mostly he watched the kids and adults that formed the Roadrunners hoping that he wouldn't do something to diminish their perception of him. Coaching was a big part of Sam Simone, providing a good experience for the players, plus giving them skills that they could use anywhere were his highest priorities. Winning would always take care of itself, learning to be both the best players possible, but also good people was his biggest challenge. Finally, Sam decided that he wasn't going to let Coben best him.

THE OLD GANG COMES HOME

"Mac let's start warming up for the game. Marie lead the team over to that open area and start stretching.

"Okay, Dad." Marie lead her teammates to the open area and began their stretching.

"Coach, do you have a minute?" Sam turned and looked at the faces of the group.

"Tad Shipley, Tavin Long, and Scooter Floyd. Wow, it's been years, what brings you guys out here today?"

"I met your son Joey in class the other day." Tad seemed to be the spokesman for the group.

"Yeah, Joey told me. Tavin nice to see you again under better circumstances. I hope that things are working out for Cindy."

"I think that things are going to be just fine for Cindy. I didn't get a chance to thank you for your part in that matter, but everything was rather hectic at the time."

"Scooter it's been a long time. You're looking fit. What are you up to these days?"

"I own, or I should say, my family owns Green Valley Technologies in Kent."

"You own Green Valley Technologies?" Mac asked with a little surprise in his voice.

"I'm sorry that I wasn't in when you came by the other day, but maybe we can all get together for lunch some time."

"That would be great. Are you guys going to stay and watch the game?"

"We wouldn't miss it for the world, especially since you're playing that prick Coben." Scooter's comment made both Sam and Mac take notice. As a kid Scooter liked everyone. So, maybe Scooter as an adult had changed. Coben had the ability to make everyone express their opinions.

"Coach, I hear that your kid is a pretty good player."

"Yeah, Marie can play, but if my memory is right all of you guys were pretty good players, too!"

"I guess it had to be the coaching." Tavin's comment got a laugh out of all the guys. Mac, Tavin, Tad, and Scooter were some of the best players that I had ever coached. They had won a lot of games playing for me. All of them then went on to play college soccer, too! The Roadrunners didn't have to take a backseat to any team, so it would be interesting to have my first team watch my current team. I guess I'm a proud papa when it comes to the kids that I've coached.

"Captains," called the ref from the center circle.

"Petty and Suzy," Mac motioned to the captains.

"Team gather in. Same lineup. Just be aggressive until we get a feel for their style."

"Sam, we defend the west goal, they kickoff." Petty announced as she and Suzy joined the group.

"Okay, let's have a good game."

"Go, Roadrunners," yelled the team as the starters ran onto the field. The girls appeared very relaxed as they took the field.

"I hope the excitement doesn't hurt the kids."

"Sam, they look ready to take on the world, so let's just see what happens." Mac commented. Mac was always able to block out the distractions when he played. This trait must help him in his job as a railroad cop.

The game started with the Roadrunners dominating the ball. The kids were moving even better than in the first game. It took just ten minutes for Suzy to slip past her defender and chip the ball into the goal. The goal brought an eruption from my old players. The guys were blasting Coben from the stands. Coben threw his clipboard down in disgust. Coben's outburst brought another round of funny and loud jeers from the anti-Coben group in the stands.

"Coach, try and keep your fans from getting too far out of hand." The referee knew that we might have some problems if they went much further with their catcalls and putdowns.

"I'll see what I can do, but those guys have a long history with Coach Coben."

"Talk to them and see if they'll cool it so we can get the game in without a riot." The ref turned around and Coben's team kicked-off for the second time in the game.

"Mac, can you see if Tavin or one of them will come and talk to me."

"Sure, but I won't guarantee any results. You know that once they get going it is almost impossible to slow them down." Mac headed into the stands and all the guys came back with him.

"What's up coach?" Tavin asked with a huge smirk on his face.

"What would you guys have done if you had a good chance to win a game or a tournament, but someone or a group went a little insane and caused the team to forfeit."

"Okay, Sam, we'll tone it down, but you have to admit we still got it. Shitheads like Coben bring out the best or the worst in all of us."

"Yes, you're all still some of the best putdown guys in middle school, but you funny guys are all over thirty, now. Just try and keep your comedy troop under control. Take your funny butts back into the stands. We have a game to win." All of them laughed and headed back into the stands.

The game continued for a few minutes before Marie slipped between two defenders and laced a shot into the corner of the net. This time the outburst came from the other side of the field. Coben kicked the bag of balls and the balls shot out of the end of the bag and went flying all over the pitch. Players were gathering and kicking balls back at Coben. As the balls returned to roost, Coben went ballistic again. He began kicking balls into the stands hitting his teams' fans and causing chaos on the far sideline. The game officials tried to restore order with little success.

"Hey Coach, that wasn't us!" Scooter Floyd's voice boomed out over the chaos. This brought an immediate reaction from our fans. The whole side was laughing. I had to restrain myself from joining in and laughing out loud. It took a few moments to restore order. As Coben's team kicked off Marie intercepted the ball and went by the surprised defense for a quick goal. The quickness of the goal stunned both sides. Coben slammed his clipboard down and stomped his feet like a petulant child.

"Mac sub in the rest of the girls."

Mac started giving directions to the subs as the ref waved them into the game. Marie, Suzie, and Petty came off the field with big grins on their faces. The girls slapped hands as they passed each other coming off and going onto the field.

"Nice job. Marie that goal was pretty good for a rookie. Take a break and we'll see about getting you back into the game later."

"Love you too, dad." Marie seemed to be floating after her stunning goal.

The rest of the game wasn't too eventful, we scored a couple more goals, and I was able to move players around and let some get some experience at different spots. Coben stood still and silent for most of the game. His players subbed themselves in and out of the game. The best part came when Scooter, Tavin, and Tad moved over to Coben's side of the field and began cheering behind him. Coben pretended that he couldn't hear them, but when the final whistle blew, Coben turned and loudly told them to F*** Off. The guys laughed and high-fived each other like they had just won the World Cup.

"Great game, but we still have a couple more before this is over. Let's go shake their hands." I said as we went to meet them on the field. The players behaved very well from both teams. As the line was moving, I hoped that the adults would do the same.

"Good game coach." I said as I extended my hand towards Coben.

"Screw you Simone. You can tell those ass-holes that I know where they live." Coben then spit on my shoe.

I went berserk. I'm not sure what came out of my mouth. All I know is that as I was about to take Coben down and do God knows what, when someone or something tackled me out of the way.

"Coben get your ass off this field. What type of person spits on someone?" It was Mac's voice. That's when I realized that Mac had reacted to the situation and ended it.

"Coach Coben you are ejected from this game and tournament." John Ross the referee was between Coben and Mac.

"Thank you, coach for defusing the situation."

Coben turned and left spewing a trail of profanities and threats in his wake. I got up and shook the grass and dirt off.

"I have been wanting to do that for years. That guy figuratively spits on all the coaches, but that's the first time I've seen him actually spit on someone. You guys must have some history. He's has been a thorn in our sides for a long time."

"Thanks, John. It was still a pretty good game. I feel for the kids on his team. No kid should have to put up with stuff like that. If only the club had taken care of the problem years ago. The club president didn't want to choose sides, so Coben stayed and I left."

"Well that club president finally retired. Patty the new president has been trying to resolve the issue. Today's outburst in front of all these witnesses might just be the straw that broke the camel's back."

"Patty Johnson is your new president." Mac asked

"Do you know Patty?"

"No, but I played with her brother Buddy. In fact, Sam coached him and the group of hecklers out here today."

"I guess it's a small world. As a kid I went to a lot of the games. Soccer kind of gets under your skin. I'd love to stay and chat, but I've got another game in twenty minutes. I'll see you guys tomorrow." With that John turned and headed to the Ref's tent.

"Would you guys like to join us at *Rome's Best Pizzeria*?"

"If it's okay with the team." Tad Shipley seemed hesitant as he answered.

"Sure, Mr. Shipley, we would love to compare notes on your legendary team and ours." Marie had a big smile on her face. Marie had always wanted to see how she and her team stacked up against Mac's team.

The drive to the pizza place was quieter than usual. I was trying to wrap my mind around all the crazy things that had happened. Normally, Marie and I would be dissecting the games and be excited after two shutouts in a tourney, but we just sat lost in our own thoughts. As we pulled into the parking lot, my mind began clearing as I scanned around looking for Jude's car. Jude had beat us to the pizza place. Marie and I walked to the entrance. *Rome's Best Pizzeria* smelled wonderful as we looked for Jude and David. David ran up and hugged my leg.

"Daddio, mom said to guide you and Marie to the tables." David made me smile. We followed him to the party room.

"I wasn't sure how many tables we needed, so I requested the party room." Jude was looking at me a little sideways.

"That's perfect. I'm not sure how many will show. We may have some extras. The chorus line from the games will be joining us."

"Who are those guys?"

"Just a few of the guys that played for me a few years ago."

"I hope they behave better here than at the soccer game." Jude gave me the 'You better take care of this or I will look'. Even I was hoping the guys found some manners or maturity on the way over.

"Daddio, over here by me." David was wildly waving his arms. I headed towards those wildly waving arms. Jack Petty intercepted me as I was coming in for a landing.

"Sam, that was a seriously scary guy. I hope you're not going to have more trouble from him. There was something very familiar about him. I decided to do some checking on him."

"The more, the merrier, I have our mutual friend looking into him, already."

"You were looking into him before the tournament. May I ask, why?"

"Jane, my ex, contacted me last week concerning a problem with Coben and her husband. She is in hiding because of whatever Coben and her husband are up to."

"Did you dig up any details?"

"Nothing about this problem. There was a lot of stuff about older crap the two had been involved in. The weird thing is that no charges have ever stuck. Coben has been a teacher all these years without a scandal."

"That is interesting. What is the husband's name?"

"Rod Jones."

"Hey guys, break it up. We need to order pizzas and drinks." Jude had taken charge.

As I sat down, I noticed that the boys had arrived and quietly sat down across from me. The ordering went smoothly. The team had a fund for parties and other group activities. We usually have a pizza party at the beginning of the year and one at the end of the season. The conversation was spirited. Most of the players and parents liked each other. Over the years a few minor issues had risen, but as a group we found a way to compromise for the good of the team. Pizzas and pitchers began arriving. I talked to almost every parent and player. As the food dwindled, people started getting ready to head out.

"Everybody, before you take off, I'll just give another reminder to be at the field by ten-thirty. If anyone needs a ride or can't make it please text or call Mac or me. Girls, you guys played very well, so let's go get a trophy tomorrow." The girls erupted with a cheer.

"You guys are very quiet. Too much excitement at the games?"

"Nah, coach, we were just showing our mature side." Scooter had a big smirk on his face.

Jude came up and gave me a kiss. She had David. "Sam, introduce me to your cheering section, before David and I head home."

"This is my wife, Jude, the little guy is David. These are the guys. This is Tavin, that's Tad, and the one on the left is Scooter." The guys politely acknowledged Jude and David. They were very respectable. It was like they had morphed into grownups. Jude and David made their way towards the door.

"Okay guys, let me know what's going on."

"What do you mean?" Scooter acted almost hurt as he replied.

"Come on, I haven't seen most of you for almost a decade, but you show up at a soccer tournament. Not just a tournament, but one where Coben has a team, too! I might be Italian, but that doesn't mean that I'm blind."

Tavin spoke this time. "We know that you're not blind or dumb. This has been planned for a while. Coben has done a lot of bad things over the years, yet he has never paid for any of his crimes. When I ran into you in Montesano, I saw how you had figured out that problem. I was impressed. The three of us have been trying to find a way to get Coben ever since he killed Buddy. Now he's involved with something big. Big enough to scare your ex-wife Jane into hiding. She seems to feel that you can help her, too!"

I sat there trying to digest everything that Tavin had said. They knew about Jane contacting me for help. I don't know if I ever thought Coben capable of murder. They seemed to believe that he was.

Mac spoke up, "Are you guys basing this on facts or just your hatred for Coben?"

"We have lots of facts, but nothing that will bring them all together. Mac, we all were involved with Coben when Buddy died. The accident was hushed up. None of us had the power or ability to get the truth out. We've been collecting information and looking for a way to bring Coben down ever since." Scooter's voice was drenched with emotion as he spoke.

"What do you mean involved with Coben?" Mac looked shocked as he asked the question.

"Mac, Sam, we aren't going to lie to anyone about are involvement with some of Coben's shady deals. No excuse for being young and dumb, but we helped Coben and that Jones guy on a number of bad deals."

"Are you talking about Rod Jones?" Sam asked.

"Yeah, do you know him?"

"No, but he's my ex-wife's husband. She contacted me last week. When I tried to call her this Jones guy answered the phone."

"Do you know where your ex is?" Tad asked a little too fast.

"That's the problem, she is in hiding. She, eventually called back on a disposable cell phone."

"We believe that she knows most of what is going on. We have proof that she is having an affair with Coben."

"She told me that. She also told me that Coben made threats against my kids. I have someone looking into Coben and Jones's backgrounds."

"Mac, we have reason to believe that the theft and accident that you're investigating will lead you to Coben."

"Scooter, why do I get the feeling that you're only telling us what you want us to hear?"

"Mac, I can only tell you what I know. Any bad publicity can harm my company. I want Coben pretty bad, but I want him for everything including Buddy's murder."

The table got quiet. Everyone at the table had something to lose or gain in the situation. Sam wasn't sure if everyone had pure motives or if there was a bigger issue not on the table.

"Scooter, I would like to talk to you about this on Monday. I can come to your office or you can come to mine. Let me know. I need to get going because I have a date."

"Mac call my office Monday morning and we'll get together and I'll sit down with you, okay?"

"Sure, that's great. Guys, I'm always glad to see all of you." Mac made his way out the door.

"It's been nice seeing all of you, but we've got an early game in the morning." Sam hugged his old players and headed to his T-Bird.

THE BLIND DATE

Mac made dinner for his grandfather. The two had shared a house for nearly ten years. This turned out to be perfect for both Jimmie Mac and Mac. Mac's parents Jimmie and Carmela lived about six blocks from Jimmie Mac's house. Mac saw his dad every day at work and between him and his parents the family helped keep Jimmie Mac in his home. Carmela loved taking care of her men.

Mac loved talking to his grandpa. He had filled him in on all of the events at the tournament. Jimmie Mac gave Mac his own advice on what to do about all of events. Basically, telling him to watch his back.

"So, you're going on a blind date. Your friend that married the guitar player set it up. I hope it works out better than the last one; the crazy one."

"You and me both, I gotta go Jimmie Mac. Call my cell if you need anything, okay?"

"Don't worry, I'll call your dad if I need anything." Mac hugged his grandpa and left.

Mac was thinking about his date during the short drive to the Big A Saloon. Jody had been playing matchmaker for him. The matchmaking had hit a few snags along the way. The worst one was the young woman that at first seemed too good to be true. Sheila had walked away from Western State Hospital. The only problem was that she couldn't maintain her touch with reality. Mac felt that he was lucky to escape with little harm, but by the time that Sheila lost it Mac wasn't sad to see her back in custody at Western State. Jody and Mac joked about what happened. Both were glad that they had dodged a bullet with little real damage to them.

Mac pulled his car into the parking lot at the Big A. The lot was nearly empty. Sam used to talk about the old dirt lot being double parked with cars making it almost impossible leave until the people that were blocking you decided to go. Mac had grown up listening to Sam and his buds telling funny stories of their escapades at the Big A. Since Jody bought the business, the place had been cleaned up to the point that nothing too outrageous had ever happened in Mac's years of going to the bar.

Music hit Mac in the face as he walked in. Not the band, just the stereo system pumping out a mix of rock and country. Mac spotted Jody and headed towards her. Passing the bar, Joe the regular bartender waved at Mac as he asked what he wanted to drink. "What're you having tonight, Mac?"

"Just a schooner of beer, Joe."

"Coming right up. Are you joining Jody?"

"To start, but you never know what's gonna happen." Both men laughed the easy laugh of friends.

"Mac, I didn't see you come in. Have a seat. Did you order?"

"Yeah, Joe's bringing me a schooner." Mac sat down and noticed that Jody looked radiant. She looked like life was really going good for her. Marriage sure looked good on her. Joe placed a coaster and Mac's beer down in front of him. Without any hesitation Mac took a long drink from his beer.

"You look like a man that just got rescued from the desert in hostile territory."

"It kind of feels that way. This week with all the craziness with Sam, work, and soccer has been taxing at best. Today, Sam and this Coben character almost came to blows when Coben spit on Sam. It took all of my strength to get them apart. In the middle of all of this stuff, a few of the guys that played with my teams showed up and started pouring fuel on the fire."

"Well, I hope that your date can put you in a better mood. Patty is very nice. I also think that you'll think she's good-looking, too! She should be here any moment."

"I just hope that she didn't just escape from Western State."

"Me too, brother." Jody and Mac laughed like school kids.

As the two friends were settling down from their giggle fest, an attractive, yet familiar woman approached the table. Jody stood up and hugged the woman. Mac sat very still as Jody turned to introduce the newcomer.

"Mac, this is Patty, Patty Johnson." Mac stood up and smiled as he realized that the Patty, he'd met at the tournament couldn't hold a candle to the gorgeous Patty standing in front of him. She was dressed in a short colorful summer dress that showed off her slim, but curvy figure. Her eyes were a brilliant green that matched her strawberry blonde shoulder length hair. Mac was lost while he drank in the Patty Johnson that was standing before him.

"Mac, earth to Mac, did I miss something?" Jody wasn't sure what was going on.

"No, Patty and I met this afternoon. I'm just having a wow moment." Mac began turning red as he reached out and touched Patty's hand.

Patty had been very quiet as she held Mac's hand. Patty was having her own wow moment. At the tournament she had barely noticed Mac. She had talked mostly to Sam. The trouble with Coben and seeing all of her brother's old friends had made her barely notice Mac, but as she looked at him now, she began to remember the shy boy that played soccer with her brother and how she had thought he was cute. He was a very nice-looking man. Dark curly hair, powerful looking without being over muscled, and a calm self-assured demeanor. Wow!

"This is weird, Jody, but Mac and I met today at the soccer tournament. We actually knew each other as kids, too!"

Hesitantly, Jody asked, "Is this good or bad?"

"Good!" Both Mac and Patty answered at the same time. Jody heaved a sigh of relief. When Jody played matchmaker, she was always worried that her matches would end in disaster. This one looked good, so far.

"I'm going to leave you two alone, so that you can get to know each other. I have to stick around for a few more hours. Let me know if you need anything, okay?"

"Sure Jody, thanks." Mac replied with a big grin on his face. Jody went back to watching over her place.

"Mac, I was pleasantly surprised to see you sitting with Jody. How long have you known Jody?"

"I don't know, maybe ten or so years. Jody and Sam go all the way back to high school. I've always felt that they had crushes on each other, but for some reason they never hooked up."

"I met Jody about five years ago. I was just getting back on my feet after a break-up. She was still mostly Queenie back then, but we hit it off and became friends."

"Tell me about yourself, it's been a long time since you used to come to our soccer games."

"It sure has. I used watch all of you guys and pretend that I wasn't interested in soccer or any of you guys, but I was a little shy and the younger sister, so I never thought that any of you would have noticed me."

"Oh, I noticed you. When we played Alpac in high school I saw you in the stands. I noticed you."

"Mac, why didn't you come over and say hi?"

"I was pretty shy myself. I'd have melted into the ground if you didn't remember me. You were very hot in high school. I'm not saying that you're not hot now because you are." Mac was nearly stammering as he talked to Patty. Patty reached across the table and squeezed Mac's hand. Mac instantly relaxed and felt as sure of himself as he ever had.

"Let's dance." As soon as the words were out of Patty's mouth, Mac was up and leading her to the dance floor. Mac wanted the night and feelings to go on forever. Patty hoped that Mac was whom he seemed to be. Patty had worried for years that she may never find Mr. Right after her nasty marriage and divorce. The dance and the night ended early because both of them had to be up early for soccer tournament.

Sam slowly climbed out of his car. The day had taken a toll on him. Every time he lifted his foot, he felt as if his shoes were made out of lead. The confrontation with Coben drained him. The unexpected appearance of his former players dusted him with another layer of intrigue. Sam stopped and picked up a few of David's toys and put them away. His movements may have been slow, but his mind was in overdrive. The inside garage door opened with a burst of energy as David came out to greet him.

"Daddio! You're home. I've been waiting for you." David leaped into Sam's arms. David was just what Sam needed.

"I'm so glad that you came out to meet me. You are the best medicine a sick man could get."

"Are you sick?" David asked with a worried look on his face.

"No, David, just tired from a long day. I meant that you always cheer me up."

"Mom says that's my job. I work really hard to cheer everyone up, but sometimes Joey and Marie make me go away. That makes me sad."

"Well, maybe I'll just have to spank them when they're mean to you."

"No daddy, I don't want them to be sad, too!"

"Wow, you're really smart. I wonder how you got so smart?"

"From you and Mommy, silly." David laughed and hugged his dad.

Sam and David danced into the house. Jude was in the kitchen cleaning. She looked up at the happy pair. "I see my little cheer up agent found you."

"He was just the right medicine for me after the strangeness at the tournament. I'm not sure what was worse, Coben or the boys. There is something else going on between them."

"I didn't get the idea that the guys were there for the games. They tried to antagonize Coben as much as they could. Coben gave them the reaction that they wanted, but I couldn't figure out why."

"They hate him because they believe that he killed Buddy Johnson. Buddy was one of my players. He died under mysterious circumstances. The guys also made some claims about a theft at the railroad that they feel that Coben and Jane's husband are involved in."

"That sounds all cloak and dagger. Did they give you any proof?"

"No, but they knew about Jane's affair with Coben and that she is in hiding."

"Are they trying to drag you into all this crap?"

"I do believe that they are. That's why I have Fatty looking into the stuff that Jane gave me and Jack Petty has also started looking at Coben. Mac has a meeting with Scooter on Monday about the theft at the railyard."

"Sometimes, it seems like you're a moth drawn to fire. Be careful. Let's try and have a quiet evening. No soccer or Coben allowed."

"Okay, I'd like that. Let's find a movie and just kick back."

Jude soon found a movie as the family gathered round to watch. Sam couldn't shake the unsettling feeling that has been his constant companion since talking to Jane earlier in the week. At the end of the movie, everyone, contentedly, made their way towards bed. Sam set his alarm for extra early.

CONFESSION IS GOOD FOR THE SOUL

Morning came too fast. Sam was moving before the alarm sounded. Quietly, Sam rolled out of bed heading towards the shower. Warm water woke Sam up making him even more determined to reach his destination. Sam was dressing as Jude woke up. Lazily, brushing the sleep from tired blue eyes, Jude sat up, giving Sam a million-watt smile.

"What gets you up at such an ungodly hour?"

"I'm going to Mass."

"You're going to seven o'clock Mass. All the crazy stuff this week must have hit you harder than I thought. Do you want company?"

"Thanks, but no. I just want a chance to talk to Eugene after Mass. He always seems to find the right words when I need them. With him being transferred I may not get too many times to talk with him." Sam reached over and embraced Jude. The embrace was followed by a kiss. It took everything Sam had to pull away from the clutch. Jude chuckled as they parted.

"You must really need to talk to Eugene." Her smile made Sam feel better as he headed towards the door.

The Thunderbird quietly turned over. Before Sam backed out of the driveway, he reached over and shut off the stereo. The morning cried for silence as Sam made his way across town to

Blessed Family. The events of the preceding week played in his head on a continuous loop.

Blessed Family loomed ahead of Sam as he slowly turned into the parking lot. This church had been his spiritual home for most of his life. Priests came and went, but the comforting feeling of the parish had never changed. Sam didn't make it to Mass every Sunday, yet he still maintained a connection to this church. Father Eugene had struck a nerve with Sam when he became the pastor over ten years ago. The two men became friends. The announcement of Eugene's pending transfer was another broadside to Sam. Sam felt like he was listing in the water, hence the early morning trip to Mass.

The parking lot was fuller than Sam thought it would be. It had been years since Sam had attended early Mass. His family came from a long line of late morning Mass attenders. The doors were open beckoning him to enter. The ushers gave Sam a warm welcome, shaking his hand, making him feel welcome. By the time that Sam reached his pew he was seeing the day in a new light.

Kneeling, Sam looked around at the familiar sanctuary. The church was built during the sixties. It had been planned with all of the changes that came out of Vatican II. The stained-glass windows were plain. The walls were very spartan having no statues and little decorations. The Stations of the Cross were carved wood and very modern looking. This was where Sam had experienced his Catholic upbringing.

The bells started tolling announcing the start of Mass. Father Eugene walked into the church from the rear with the altar servers, lay readers, and the eucharistic ministers. Early Mass was usually the fastest service because of the smaller number of attendees.

"The Mass is over. Go in peace." Father Eugene then made the procession towards the vestibule. Sam waited until most of the people had walked out before he headed out.

"Well, Sam, I'm not sure that my heart can handle such a shock as seeing you at seven o'clock Mass."

"Very funny. I think that I'm going to miss your razor wit." Eugene grabbed Sam and hugged him tight. Emotion filled the priest's eyes as he held his friend.

"I suppose you're here to talk about your horrible week?"

"Yes, you're right. The parish hotline is still functioning." Both men laughed and started walking towards the sacristy.

"I'm not sure about how much of what I heard is true or exaggerations."

Sam snorted, "I bet it's pretty close to the truth. I've had a horrendous week."

"Why don't you give me an overview of your week and I'll see if I can help."

Sam and Eugene talked for nearly an hour. Sam did most of the talking. Eugene listened.

"That's my week in a nutshell. I just know that dealing with Jane and Coben in the same week has made me feel like a bomb waiting to explode."

"I don't know whether to laugh or cry. What person wouldn't react badly to having their biggest disappointments resurrected in the flesh. Whatever places you had sent these memories must have opened the door flooding you with all those bad memories. I think, knowing you, that everything will settle down. The soccer tournament ends today and Jane will soon find someone else to hold her attention."

Sam exhaled. "I know that you're right, but something is still nagging from deep inside. I'm not sure that everything has happened, yet."

"You'll just have to have faith. Look at the time. You better get going. I know how early you want to be there for the first game."

"Thanks, Eugene, I hope that we can still get together after you leave. You can't have too many friends."

PART 4

THE PLOT THICKENS

The door to the storage shed was open. A solitary man stepped out pushing a cart. The cart was loaded down with nets and field markers. The man placed the markers at the corners of each field. The nets were put up next. Soon, all the fields were ready for the games. The man made his way back to the shed. He whistled an old tune as he pushed the empty cart. The cart was placed into the shed and the door was relocked. The man headed back to his car when he saw a man approaching.

"Well, if it isn't Coach Coben. You looked like you were really enjoying yourself."

"What are you doing here? You're not supposed to contact me in person." Coben's face betrayed his fear. They had never come to him in the open like this.

"We thought that you and your partners needed a reminder as to who was running this show. Jones seems to have disappeared, also I warned you about the woman. She has made contact with her ex. On the surface this looks bad for you. The merchandise hasn't been delivered, either."

"The merchandise is in a safe place, as to my so-called partners they don't matter. I finish what I start. Jones never knows the whole deal and Jane was never part of this. Who gives a shit about her contacting Simone? He's a loser. I've got everything under control." Coben began to feel confident. He wasn't going to back down from anyone.

"That's not how we see it. It's my job to clean up loose ends. Coben, you're the biggest loose end in this deal." The man had a gun in his hand. Coben started backing away. The man shot Coben as he backed away. Coben was dead as he hit the ground.

A few minutes later the man walked back towards his car. Coben's body was hidden under some tarps.

The man started his car and reached for his phone. "The cleanup has started. It will not blow back on us. I am still trying to track the other two. I'll keep you informed." The call ended as the man exited the park.

Sam grabbed the box of muffins that he bought on the way home from Mass when a whirling dervish jumped him from behind. "Daddio, you brought muffins. Hurry up. You don't want to be late for the game; do you?"

"David, who let you out of your cage?"

"I don't live in a gage. You know that." David laughed as he was hugging and running around Sam. They were soon safely inside the house.

"Muffins, I brought muffins. Get one before they're gone." The rest of the family made their way into the kitchen for a muffin.

"Mass or Eugene must have been good for you this morning." Jude gave Sam a kiss on his cheek.

"Yes, I think it was good for me. I'll tell you about it later, but we've got muffins to eat before the big game today."

"Momma, Daddio, said that I live in a cage. I don't live in a cage. Do I?"

"Sam, stop teasing that boy. David should I punish him?"

"Not now, maybe after the games."

"Yeah, Mom after the games," both Marie and Joey chimed in.

The muffins were soon devoured. Sam and Marie got ready to head out to the fields for the game. The rest of the family would go to the game closer to the starting time. Team warm-ups were for hardcore fans or away games. Mac had texted Marie telling her that he wouldn't need a ride.

"Dad, Mac doesn't need a ride. Do I need to put anything in your car?"

"No, I left all the gear in from yesterday. Do you have your water bottle?"

"Yep, right here. I'm ready, if you are." Marie went out the front door.

"Sam, what field is the first game on?" Jude asked as she walked into the living room.

"Field #3 for the first game. The next game depends on if we win or lose." Sam kissed Jude and David.

"Joey is bringing Ginger. Promise that you won't tease him, okay?"

"I'm shocked to think that anyone thinks I would tease my son." Sam went to the door with a smile. He was a dad feeling pride at the idea that his oldest had a girlfriend.

Marie was already in the Thunderbird when Sam climbed in. Sam guided the car out of the driveway. "Why are you smirking like that? What's going on?"

"I'm not smirking. I'm just feeling good about Joey. Can't a dad feel good about his children?"

"Jude must have told you that Joey's bringing Ginger to the games." Marie punched her dad on the arm.

"I suppose, that I was the last to know about this."

"For cripe's sake, Dad, Joey has been walking on air for a week. He's had the hots for Ginger forever."

The two rode in amused silence for the next few minutes. Marie and Sam made many trips to soccer games together. They sometimes talked the whole ride to the games or they rode in silence. Today, was a combination of the two. Marie loved soccer, but she loved that she shared it with her dad.

The entrance to Alpac Fields loomed just down the road. Sam started checking out the parking lot to see if his team was early or if it would be game time before he knew what his lineup looked like. Marie always looked for the other teams to see how they stacked up. They both spotted Mac at the same time. Mac was talking to Patty Johnson. Sam soon found a parking spot near the concession stand.

"Let's get the gear unloaded. Then we'll double check to see which field that we're playing on."

"Okay, Dad. I see Suzie, I'll get her to help me haul the stuff." Marie started waving at Suzie and her dad. The pair headed towards the car. Sam made his way towards Mac and Patty.

"You're extra early, today." Sam greeted Mac as he walked up.

"You know me, I like to be prepared for everything that I do." Both, Sam and Mac cracked up laughing.

"So, you two must have had a good time last night?"

"Wait a minute, you knew that Patty was my blind date?"

"I didn't then, but I do now." Sam was smirking as Mac's face started turning red.

"You know, Buddy used to say that you could read people's minds. I think maybe he was right." Patty was all smiles as she looked at Mac and Sam.

"Okay, Mac, let's go win this tournament." Sam turned and headed towards the field. Mac gave Patty a hug and followed.

PLAY BALL

"Let's start with some stretching. Marie and Suzie lead the team. Mac, when their done stretching grab April and put her through some keeper drills." The team jumped right into their pregame warm-ups. Sam filled out his line-up card. It was an easy task when everyone had made it on time. Sam used this time to reflect on his choices as far as lineups and strategies. They were playing the Kickers. The Kickers were in the same league as the Roadrunners, so the teams knew each other very well.

"Coach, I'll need your player cards in about ten minutes." The referee turned and quickly headed to the other sideline.

"Mac, bring them in. Ladies bag up the gear. If you have to go, do it now." Balls and players started bombing the sideline. Every player had their own way of getting ready for games. Most of the Roadrunner girls had played soccer for years, so they were set in these rituals. Sam had his own pre-game quirks. Sam tried to have the same routine before every game. As a player, Sam knew that inconsistent coaches could trip teams up. The more consistent everyone was, usually made for more consistent play.

"Gather in, everybody. The ref will be here in few minutes. Does anyone have any questions or problems?"

"What's the line-up?" Suzie asked. Sometimes Suzie was nervous at the beginning of games. I used to sit her for the first five minutes. This helped her a lot with pre-game jitters, but she had got over most of the nervous stuff as she got older.

"Suzie, call the lineup." Suzie quickly called out the starting lineup as the Referee walked up.

"Coach, have your players give me their numbers when I call their names." This came off with no problems. "Have a good game." The ref then headed back to the center circle. The team captains followed.

"We kick-off and defend the south goal." Petty called as her and Marie came off the field.

"Does everyone know the lineup? Okay, let's just play our game. We know this team and they know us. Look for the open lanes and push them. Gather in."

"On three, go Roadrunners." Petty and Suzie led the pre-game cheer. As the cheer ended the starters ran onto the field.

The game was close, but anti-climactic. The Roadrunners held on to post a 3-2 victory that put them in the championship game. The other semi-final game was just starting. Most of the players headed to the concession stand for a snack or a restroom break. Sam and Mac followed behind the team talking about the game.

"It wasn't pretty, but they hung in and held them off." Mac seemed off, a little, this morning. Maybe it was the game or maybe it was Patty.

"There were some good things. I think that the whole squad contributed to the victory, but either they took them for granted or were a little tired from yesterday. We might need to push them harder in training." Sam was enjoying watching the kids interacting at the concession stand.

"Well, Coach, it was still a win. Do you know much about the other two teams?" Jack Petty asked as Fred Barr as some of the other parents came up. Sam laughed to his self. When he started coaching these kids, most if not all of the parents, didn't know a penalty kick from a head ball. The parents had learned right along with their kids.

"I don't know very much about either team. We may have even played them before, but I don't remember. We'll get a little knowledge by watching them play."

"Take a break, coach. We're going to head back and watch the game." With that said, Fred and the rest of the parents went back to watch the game. The girls had bought some snacks and were already watching the game.

"Thanks, Fred, I think that I'll do just that." Sam was looking around for Jude and the boys. He soon spotted them at the younger kids' playground. Sam turned to tell Mac where he was headed, but Mac was in conference with Patty.

"Here comes Daddio!" David yelled loud enough for the whole park to hear. David came off the top of the climber and sprinted towards his dad.

"Wow, that's quite the greeting." David leaped into Sam's arms. They went down in a heap. Sam and David laughed and giggled as they hit the ground. David brightened Sam's spirit every time he laughed and squirmed. Jude helped the duo up and gave them a brilliant smile.

"Sam, are you still in one piece?"

"Nothing is broken. That boy is going to be a linebacker someday. Did you meet Joey's girl?"

"Yes. She seems very nice, plus she is gorgeous."

"Well, Simone men have good taste in women. Present company included." Sam was grinning ear to ear.

"Compliments will save you this time." Jude gave Sam a kiss on his forehead.

"Where is Joey?"

"They're sitting on the other side of the park. I guess they wanted a little privacy."

Mac went back to the concession stand. Mac's mind wasn't on soccer this morning. He couldn't get his mind off of Patty. The feelings that he was having hadn't showed up for a long time. Patty was talking to some people when see noticed Mac standing there.

"Okay, I'll get a new corner flag for Field #3. Thanks for letting me know." The people walked away as Patty stepped towards Mac.

"What's up?"

"One of the players broke or bent a corner flag. I need to get it replaced before the next game."

"I'll get it for you. Where are they kept?"

"That would be great. See that building on the other side of the last field, we keep them inside on the right. Here's the key in case its locked." As Patty handed Mac the keys, she kissed him. Mac was surprised. Not only was it a great kiss, it was a great kiss. Mac was a very happy man as he walked to the storage building.

The doors were on the far side of the building. Mac made his way around to the doors when he noticed something unusual on the side area. It looked like someone had moved junk around. Mac's police instincts started twitching. As he approached the pile, he zeroed in on a foot sticking out of the bottom of the pile. Mac backed away; he didn't want to contaminate what was very likely a crime scene. Mac pulled his cell phone out and called Sam.

Sam's phone started ringing in Jude's purse. "Sam, your phone is ringing."

"Hello, Sam here."

"Sam, I need you to get Jack Petty and come over to the storage building, but just you two, okay."

"Sure Mac, what's wrong?"

"It's better if you two just come quietly and everything will become clear."

"What's wrong, Sam?"

"I'm not sure, but Mac needs me and Jack to help him at the storage building."

Sam walked over to Jack Petty. Jack was in a group of parents relaxing and watching the other semi-final game.

"Jack can I have a word with you?"

"Sure." Jack stepped over to Sam. Sam quickly told him what Mac had said. The two men quietly moved from the group. Neither spoke as they walked. The men turned the corner of the storage building to find Mac standing very still and looking at the pile.

"Jack would you look at the pile over there." Mac pointed at debris on the side of the building. Jack and Sam moved to the pile and scanned the area.

"Mac have you called anyone else?"

"No, I wanted to have you verify that we have a body. I have never worked a possible homicide before." Jack pulled his cell out and called 911.

"Sam, would you go back and get the tournament director."

"Sure, Jack right away." Sam was relieved to go for Patty. Mac and Jack stayed to protect the scene.

As Sam approached Patty, he motioned for her to come over. Patty looked puzzled.

"What do you need Sam?"

"There is a problem at the storage building. Jack and Mac need you to come there."

"A problem, what type of problem?" Soccer players and fans moved all around them. Sam was trying to be discreet in the middle of the mass of people.

"You'll see when we get there."

THE UNVEILING

The tournament continued unaware of the trouble just around the corner. Patty and Sam turned the corner. Patty surveyed the scene puzzled by what she saw. Chief Petty and Mac stood by the pile on the back side of the storage building.

"Mac, what's going on?" Patty sounded nervous, not alarmed.

"Patty, take a look at the pile." Mac and Sam moved closer to Patty as she stepped forward and looked. "Oh my God, is that a body?" Patty started to sag, but recovered quickly.

"Yes," Chief Petty answered.

"Who is it? Why haven't you dug him out?"

"Patty, we're waiting for the police. This is most likely a crime scene." Mac put his arm around Patty. No one seemed to know proper procedures for a crime scene.

"You may need to talk to the police when they get here, meanwhile we don't want to panic the people at the tournament." Sam talked in a calm reassuring voice. Sam was becoming a veteran of these kind of events.

The four turned as one when they heard a car pulling up at the building. The Alpac police had arrived. The police cruiser stopped and two officers emerged. The pair moved towards them.

"Where is the body?" The older of the two officers asked.

"Right there at corner of the pile." Chief Petty stepped aside and pointed. The officers squatted down and examined the area.

"Who found the body?"

"I did." Mac held out his badge and ID.

"You're a Special Agent?"

"I'm the Special Agent in Charge for the Cascade and Pacific Railroad."

"Sir, your identification, please." The officer pointed at Chief Petty.

"I'm Chief Jack Petty of the Twin Rivers Police." Jack said has he handed the officer his identification. The officer had a puzzled look when turned towards Sam.

"Sam Simone," Sam quietly added.

"I'm Patty Johnson. I am the tournament director."

"Your names, please." Jack asked the officers.

"I'm Sgt. Bob James and this is Officer George Bancroft, Chief. Can someone give me an idea of what took place this morning?"

"I arrived at eight this morning to oversee the setup for today's tournament. The fields had to be marked and the nets hung, plus whatever else needed to be fixed for the games. Most of the work had already been done, so we just completed the fields. There were four of us here working."

"Did anyone open the storage building?"

"Yes, Tom and Joe, they do the field preps." Sgt. James wrote notes as Patty talked. Cheers could be heard from the fields.

"Are they still here?"

"Yes, they are involved in many things during the games and they also, remove the nets and flags after the games end."

"Can you quietly find them and bring them back?" Patty agreed and started back to the fields. More official vehicles began pulling up. Soon, it would be hard to keep the scene under wraps.

"George, I want you to interview Mr. Simone. I'll talk to Chief Petty and Special Agent Delac."

"Right this way, Mr. Simone." Officer Bancroft pointed towards his police car. Sam followed him to the car. "I've wanted to meet you for a while, Sam, is it okay to call you Sam?"

"Yes, I'd rather you called me Sam. Mr. Simone is too formal." This seemed to break the ice between Sam and the officer.

"I'll need your full name and address." Sam gave him the information. "Why are you here today."

"I coach the Roadrunners. The team played in the semi-final game this morning. We are waiting for the other semi-final to finish to find out what team we'll be playing for the championship."

"What time did you arrive this morning?"

"The game was scheduled for ten, so I arrived at about 9:15."

"Can anyone verify that?"

"My daughter, Mac, and my wife can. There were also a few other players and parents here, too!"

"Okay, I'll follow up with them. Can you tell me what happened?"

"Let me see, at the end of our game we went to the concession stand to see when our next game would start and to relax between games. Patty Johnson, the tournament director, asked Mac to go the storage building to get replacement flags for one of the fields. I was talking to my wife when my phone rang. Mac called to ask me to bring Jack Petty over to the storage building. When we got there, Mac showed us the body. Jack Petty told me to get Patty and he called 911. I found Patty and we returned to the scene."

"Do you have any idea who the victim is?"

"No." The answer kind of hung in the air. We moved back toward the body. The medical examiners were on the scene when we returned.

I found Mac and we watched the technicians work. They still hadn't uncovered the body. Pictures were being taken from every angle. Measurements and notes were recorded. The techs didn't want to miss anything at the scene.

After, what seemed like hours, the techs and detectives started the process of uncovering the body. There were too many people blocking our view to see much at this point. Sgt. James turned and waved us over. As a group we moved towards the body.

"Do any of you know this person?"

"That's Rick Coben." We answered as a group.

"All of you know the victim? Okay, we'll start with you Chief Petty, tell us how you know Rick Coben."

"I met him for the first time, yesterday, he was one of the coaches. He, it seems, had a history with Sam, Mac, and Patty. There was an argument between Sam and Mr. Coben between games."

"What type of an argument?"

"The type that people have when they really don't like each other. It almost got physical, but Mac and I stepped in."

"Can the rest of you verify what the Chief said?"

"I can. Coben and I go back a long way. We coached together for a couple of miserable years when Mac and Patty's brother played on the team. Seeing him in person brought out the worst in me and I lost my cool. The Chief and Mac ended the situation. I felt pretty shitty about losing my composure in front of the players and their families."

"Mac, Patty is this what went down?"

"Yes, Sgt, just as they've told you." The medical examiner came over and pulled Sgt James aside.

"Mr. Simone where were you this morning from seven to eight?"

"I went to Mass at Blessed Family in Auburn."

"Can anyone verify that you were at Mass?"

"Sure, Father Eugene. I spent an hour talking to him about my behavior yesterday and last week."

"I think that I've got everything that I need now. Make sure that we have any contact information. Mr. Simone we will be checking out your statements. I don't see any reason that the tournament can't go on, just keep people from this area. We'll be working here for a few more hours."

The group made its way back towards the fields. I can only speak for myself, but soccer wasn't high on my priority list at the moment. As we approached the concession stand the game on the field ended. A decision had to be made by the adults involved. Finish the tournament or disappoint the kids.

"As the tournament director I think that we need to talk to the coaches and parents before deciding. Coach, can we have a word with you and your assistants?"

"Sure, Patty, what's up?"

"Let's step over here, so we can have a little privacy." Both team's coaches followed Patty. "There has been an incident here today that we need to discuss. A body was found behind the storage building. The police are treating it as a homicide. I would like to hear your thoughts on what we need to do, before I decide about the tournament."

"Someone, was murdered behind the storage building, do we know who it was?"

"There has been a tentative identification. I don't think I'm supposed to give out that information."

"Patty, what are you suggesting?" Mac quietly asked.

"I think that for the safety of the players and parents that both teams will be co-champions. This way we can let the police investigate without a park full of people."

"Coach, it's alright with me. How about you?" Sam took a moment before he replied.

"I think it is a good idea. Maybe we can set up a game to replace this one."

"That would be great. Call me and we'll work out the details."

Patty gathered all the players and parents to make an announcement and hand out the trophies. The park slowly emptied. Soon, only Sam, Mac, Patty, and a few players remained. The day had started on a high note, but crashed to the ground with the discovery of Coben's body.

"Patty do you need help cleaning up around here?" Sam looked at a very stressed tournament director. It was Mac that replied.

"Sam, I'll help Patty with the cleanup. Take the kids home and I'll stop by later."

"Okay. I'll talk to you later. Come on girls let's get the gear in the car and head home." Marie and Suzy gathered up the gear and somberly walked to the car.

"Hang in there, Patty." Sam gave Patty a big hug.

The T-Bird passed all of the police vehicles as they left the park. Not a word had been uttered until the car left the park.

"Did they know who was killed, dad?" Marie had a quiver in her voice as she spoke.

"Yes, it was Coach Coben."

"It was that nasty man from yesterday." Suzy was on the verge of tears.

"Yes. I don't know much about what happened except that the police think he was killed early this morning."

"Who found him dad?"

"Mac found him when he went to get some flags out of the storage building."

The rest of the ride was pretty quiet. When Sam pulled up in front of Suzy's house her dad was outside working in the front yard. Suzy jumped out of the car and ran to her dad. She gave him a big bearhug and ran into the house.

A startled Fred came over to the car. "Thanks, Sam, did something happen after we left the tournament?"

"There was an incident that cut the tourney short. A body was found behind the storage building. The police and the tournament director decided to end the tourney. They decided to declare us and the other team co-champions. It was a very stressful ending for all of the people that were there."

"Someone was killed. It didn't happen in front of the girls?"

"No, Fred, the person was killed sometime before the tournament started today."

"It still had to be pretty scary for everyone. I better go in and take care of my daughter. Thanks again, Sam." Fred turned and headed in to comfort his daughter. Sam reached over and squeezed Marie's hand.

MORE INTRIQUE

The woman parked the car down the block from her house. She crossed into the alley. Slowly, making her way towards the house. Nothing seemed to be out of the ordinary as she walked to the back door. She just wanted to grab a few things. Planning to get out before Rod came home. The back door opened without using her key. She had lectured Rod about making sure the doors were locked, but he either forgot or just plain ignored her. The kitchen looked clean as she made her way through it to the living room. The house was dark. In the darkness she tripped on something in the hallway. A scream escaped from her as she realized that the something was her husband. Rod was dead. The blood was dry around him. She ran out the back door and sprinted to her car.

The Simone house was rather subdued. No one, Sam included, knew what to say about the events of the weekend.

Most of the time after a game Sam and Marie would rehash how the team played, but all of the usual routines had taken a backseat to the murder. Everyone, but Joey was sitting in the family room watching or pretending to watch television.

"Dad, come to the door, please." Joey yelled from the kitchen. Sam gave Jude a quizzical look.

"Be right there." Sam headed to the back of the house.

"Dad, there's someone at the door for you."

"Who is it?"

"It's mom. I just panicked and called for you."

"That's okay, Joey. I'll see what she wants." Sam opened the door to see a visibly upset Jane standing there. "Come in." Sam ushered Jane into the kitchen.

"Sam, who is it?" Jude called from the other room.

"It's Jane." Sam answered. The kitchen soon filled up with a very curious family.

"Have a seat. Would you like something to drink or eat?" It looked like Jane was ready to run, but something kept her feet still.

"Sam, I don't know if I can talk in front of everyone." Jane was shaking as she talked.

"I'll take the kids back to the family room." Jude was watching the situation very intently.

"No, everyone needs to hear what she has gotten us into. First off, why are you here?"

"I didn't know where else to go. I went home to get some things and I found Rod dead. Someone killed him. Panic set in and I ran out the door and drove here. I can't think. I'm scared out of my wits." Jane started sobbing. Jude walked over and put her arms around her. Holding her until the sobs subsided. I knew that Jane would be the next target. It wouldn't be safe for any of us if Jane stayed here.

"Are you sure he was dead?" Jane shook her head.

"Jane, Rick Coben was found dead this morning at the soccer fields." Jane started sobbing again, but she settled down fairly quick from the second set of bad news.

"I'm scared. I told them that this job felt wrong. Rick always thought that he could out think or out smart anyone."

"Jane, did you call the police when you left your house?" Sam knew the answer, but he needed to hear it from Jane.

"No, I just freaked and ran."

"Do you have a throw-away phone." Jane took a phone out of her bag. "Okay, call the police and tell them what you found." Jane started punching in the numbers. Sam made a call on his phone.

"Mac, it's Sam, could you come over to my house it's about your case and the murders."

"Did you say murders? I'll be right there."

"Let's go into the family room. It might be more comfortable." Sam and Jude helped a very unsteady Jane into the room. The kids followed.

"Daddio, who is the lady? I've never met her before." David wasn't sure what was happening, but he knew that the lady must be someone important.

"David, come here and I'll introduce you. David this is Jane. Jane this is David. Jane is Joey and Marie's other Mom."

"Nice to meet you, Jane. I always wanted to meet Joey and Marie's other mom. I can't remember my other mommy and daddy." David gave Jane a big hug. David was working his charm on the still miserable Jane. I wouldn't have bet that Jane responded to David, but he was very powerful. Jane wiped her face and sat up.

"Marie would you take David to bed? It is already past his bedtime."

"Sure, dad, come on David. Maybe I'll read you a story." David and Marie headed towards his room. Joey came back in the room with coffee and refreshments. He handed a cup of coffee to Jane. He set the rest on the coffee table. It was odd watching Joey and Marie fighting their emotions. The reality of Jane sitting in the family room must have been a big shock for them. I wanted to comfort them, but even I was lost as to what the proper etiquette is in this situation. Jude was sitting there drinking in the scene. She had not said much since Jane had landed in our home. A car pulled into the driveway. Mac was soon in the room waiting to find out what was going on. Marie had rejoined the group when Mac arrived.

"Mac, Jane found her husband this afternoon. Someone had killed him. Rick had threatened Jane and the kids. The boys at the game Saturday, mentioned that Rick and Rob were involved in the robbery at the railyard. From what was said Scooter's family owns Green River Technology."

"That's right, they are competing for a large government contract with another local firm. The winning company will be set up for a long time. The loser may not survive. Those guys and Patty's brother Buddy all helped Coben out on his scams. Scooter believes that Coben left Buddy to die. There are many different angles to this thing. I'm trying to sort everything out so I have somewhere to look for the answers."

"Jane, what do you know about Rick and Rod's involvement in this mess?"

"Sam, it seemed like they deliberately left me out of this deal. Any other time I was an active participant in their deals."

"You were involved in criminal activities?" Marie had a look of disappointment on her face.

"Sadly, yes I was. But, none of this should come as any surprise. I'm sure your dad has said enough about me."

"What are you talking about? Dad's never said much of anything about you or why you guys split-up."

"Geez, Jane, dad stayed and helped us through our sadness. We just wanted to talk to you or see you on our birthdays. Dad did double duty until Jude came into our lives. We missed you and inwardly never stopped hoping that you would appear in our lives again. As the years went by, we pushed our thoughts of you into our memories going on with the business of growing up. That's what dad gave us even though he was hurting as much or more than we were."

Everyone turned and looked at Joey as he made what may have been the longest speech he'd ever given. I was proud of my son. He didn't tear Jane down, but he let the world know what he felt and what he was made of. Marie put her arm around her big brother and lightly kissed his cheek.

"Maybe this was a mistake to come here and open these wounds. I'll just go." Jane started to get up.

"Sit down, right now. You're not going anywhere until we find a safe place for you to go. You called Sam because he would help you, but you forget or just don't know what Sam is made of. No one is going to let you leave if there is even a small chance of these guys getting to you. So, shut up and stop feeling sorry for yourself." That's my girl. Jude had backbone to spare. We needed a plan to put Jane in a safe place and draw out the killers.

"Sam, remember the cabin on Jimmie Mac's farm?"

"Yeah, is it livable?"

"Who's Jimmie Mac?" Jane asked.

"Jimmie Mac is my grandfather. He had the place remodeled a couple of years ago. I stay there once in a while. It's small but comfortable."

"Where is your car? We need to put it somewhere out of sight."

"It's on the street behind the house."

"Give me your keys. Mac will take you to the farm. Do you need anything? I think that the car will be safe at Good Samaritan's. Joey meet me at Good Sam's."

"I'll need a change of clothes from the car and some food." Jane looked dubious about the plan. I was dubious about the plan, but it was the best we had at the moment.

DUBIOUS PLANS

Everyone involved in the logistics of hiding Jane and her car grabbed what was needed. We began to leave. Sam had run to Jane's car to retrieve her things. Joey backed the Thunderbird out and headed to Good Sam's. Jane and Mac waited until Sam and Joey had left before starting to the door.

"Wait a minute, Jane. I need to say something." Jude reached out and touched Jane's arm. Jane stopped and turned toward Jude.

"I wasn't around when you and Sam were together, but I know that he still cares about you deep inside. His is an open wound. It heals a little more each year, but I have never heard him utter a bad word about you. This week has been incredibly hard on him. Seeing you and being placed in the middle of this mess has hit him hard. The kids were upset when he told them you had come to see him. He was worried about how I would react to your reappearance, yet he still helped you. I know that you were his first love. I also know that I'm his last love. He or I would never let you drown. If we could save you. When this is over, I want you to try and repair some of the damages you have caused with the kids. I love them and will do anything for them."

"I don't know what to say. I'm a mess, but I know there is love in this house. I felt it the moment I crossed the threshold. If

I survive, I would like to get to know you and the kids. Thank you."

Jane went out to Mac's car. Mac opened the door so that Jane could climb in. The two didn't say anything for a few minutes. Jane wasn't sure where they were going. She had never heard of or been to Jimmie Mac's farm. Mac headed towards the upper Green River Valley. At the Neeley Mansion, Mac took a right and followed the road towards Flaming Geyser.

"Mac, I know that we never got along very well when Sam and I were married, but I do appreciate you helping me. When all of this started, I didn't know or have anyone else to turn to. I was afraid that I'd burned too many bridges for Sam to help. Again, I was wrong about your cousin." Mac turned and stared at Jane when she finished talking.

"Jane, I didn't like the way you treated him. I'm very close to Sam. He's the brother I didn't have. He has only talked about it a couple of times. You made him sad. He loved you deeply. It has taken him a long time to heal. I'm not sure that you know why things happened the way they did. But Sam and my mother have always said once family always family. That includes you, but you better not hurt him again."

"I never wanted to hurt him. I am not sure that I understand why I've done the things that I've done, but hurting Sam and the children is something that I can't explain or undo." The pair rode in silence the rest of the way.

Mac turned his car onto a gravel road that split some fir trees. The path was only about a half-mile long. The trees parted exposing an old- time house and a small red barn. Jane would have never suspected that unmarked road would lead to a picture from the olden days.

"Wow, it's so peaceful and serene. I didn't know that your Grandpa had a farm."

"There's a lot that you never bothered to learn, but I know that our family can be overwhelming. You missed out on some good people and memories." Jane stared at Mac. Jane had never told anyone, especially on Sam's side of the family that she didn't want to be too close to anyone. It would have complicated leaving when she left. Jane started to get out of the car.

"Stay in the car. I need to check out the property before you come in." With that said, Mac began walking around the house. Mac disappeared around the back of the house. It seemed like ages before Jane was relieved to finally see Mac open the front door waving her in.

As Jane walked through the front door, she noticed that the small house was clean and simply decorated. "Mac, this place is wonderful. Is everything in order?"

"It seems to be or otherwise I wouldn't have let you in." Mac went out and retrieved Jane's stuff. Mac gave Jane a quick tour and explained how everything worked. He gave her a list of numbers for both him and Sam. It was late when Mac drove back out the long gravel road.

CONSPIRATORS

The men were gathered around a table in Scooter's private office. Fear and worry hung in the air. None of the men had signed on for what had happened that day. No conversation filled the room. Scooter told them that they would soon know the details of the problem. Each of the men had been friends since childhood. They had all survived many adventures together, but today had passed a line that could ruin each of them. The phone rang. Scooter answered.

"Yes, we are all here. I understand, come back." Scooter set the phone down. A few moments later the door opened. Paul Layton stepped in.

"Good, I'm glad that all of you could make it. Gentlemen, I'm going to update you on the changes that took place yesterday."

"You call killing two men a change." Tavin was trying to control his voice.

"Now, counselor don't accuse me of anything without thinking through all of the consequences." Layton smiled at Tavin.

"Paul, what did happen? I thought that everyone was on the same page. Coben and his cohort would be exposed and we would win the contract. What changed?" Scooter was on the verge of hysteria.

"Coben was a loose cannon. When you and your gang of dopes set him off at the tournament it was clear that we couldn't trust him. There is a lot of money at stake, so someone needed to be on top of things, lastly the players have changed."

"What do you mean the players have changed?" Scooter looked at Tavin and Tad.

"I no longer take orders from you. If you don't believe me call this number." Scooter looked at the phone and recognized the number. He had been betrayed by his family. Scooter slumped into his chair. The room erupted into a symphony of noise.

"I'm not sure that I understand. I got involved with a plan to expose Coben, not murder." Tad felt his world crumbling.

"Everyone, settle down. If you want to get out of this in one piece, you'll do exactly what I say. No more talk of Coben. No helping Agent Delac or his cousin Sam. Let the authorities and me fix the problems. Try to go on as if nothing happened this weekend. Remember that I'll be watching all of you." Layton turned and left the room. The old friends sat defeated and weary after listening to Layton. Scooter didn't doubt that his family would harm all of them.

"Scooter, what are you going to do? Mac is coming to see you tomorrow." Tavin wasn't too worried about Layton's threats because he could disappear anytime. He was worried about his friends. This included Mac and Sam. Tavin could make himself scarce when a case got too hot, but the others couldn't just pick up and go. He needed to call in some markers to help them.

"I'm going to talk to him, but not give him any information. Tad just go to work and let me try and figure something out."

"If you say so, but I'm just plain scared. This was supposed to be about bringing Coben to justice for what he did to Buddy and us as kids. How much money is this contract worth?"

"It could be worth over two billion dollars. My family would be set for life. That's a lot of motive for all of this." The men quietly left the meeting.

Tavin went to his office. He opened a safe in the back room. The box he pulled out was carefully set on the desk. Two items were taken from the box. The first was an electronic scanner. The second was a burner phone. Tavin scanned the office. It was clean. He punched in a number on the phone.

"Hello, Mac speaking."

"Mac, this is Tavin. I need to talk with you about the murders."

"I'm listening." Tavin went on to fill Mac in on all of the details that had come to light at Scooter's office.

"I'm pretty sure that Scooter's family has double-crossed him through Paul Layton. Layton threatened us during the meeting. The meaning was clear. I'm a big boy. I can make myself scarce. But, the rest of the guys can't. Can we work together to keep everyone safe?"

"Yes, just keep your head down. Sam and I are already looking into this because they have made threats against Sam's ex and the kids. I will keep my appointment with Scooter. Sam has someone checking the backgrounds on this, so I'll give him Layton's and Scooter's name. Call me tomorrow night. We'll compare notes."

The line went dead.

DIGGING IN

Sam texted some information to Fatty. Fatty confirmed the information before he started his checking. Sam called Mac to let him know that Fatty was on the job.

"That's great, Sam. We need as much ammunition as we can gather before we take on Layton and Scooter's family. I still want to look at Coben's guilt in Buddy's death."

"I already have Fatty and Chief Petty looking into the accident investigation of Buddy's death."

"It would make things smoother if there is a connection between Buddy's death and the double cross from Scooter's family. I just can't see any, yet." Mac knew that there had to be something, but he couldn't put his finger on it.

"There has to be some link between Coben and the family. I think that I'll add a little more to Fatty's investigation. Coben may have been doing dirty work for the family or the company. Knowing Coben, he probably stepped on too many toes, but unless we find the link, we can't fill in the holes. Be careful, Mac."

"You too, cuz."

Morning dawned the same as always. The house was quiet and cool. Sam gave Jude a squeeze before heading to the shower. Sam was lost in thought as he toweled off. His world had changed in a single week. He needed to be at the top of his game to find the answers to keep his family safe. The bathroom door blew open as a small tornado came through it.

"Daddio, mom says come and get it." David's face was smiling as bright as a beacon. The little tornado was packed with energy this morning.

"Tell mom that I'll be right there. I just need to put pants on."

"Yeah, you better put pants on or you'll scare the neighbors." David laughed with delight. God, he was turning into his smart-aleck older siblings, but I love it.

The kitchen smelled of pancakes. I love pancakes. Hugging the chef as I sat down.

"I thought pancakes might be just the right way to start your day. Remember, I have a meeting tonight, so I'll be late. You'll need to get David at daycare." Jude was in constant motion. A full day gave her an extra step it seemed.

"I asked Joey to pick up David. I'll try to be out of work a little early. Don't worry about us, okay?"

"Look who's telling me not to worry. You're the King of worry. Give me a kiss before I'm late. David give your father a kiss. Hurry up."

Kisses were exchanged. At last I was alone. I had a few minutes before I needed to leave, so I made sure every door and window was closed. I went over what I had to do today, both work related and Coben related. It's not a long drive to work, but I couldn't tell you one thing that I passed on the way in. It surprised me to see that I wasn't the first person in the parking lot. I didn't recognize the other car.

"Are you Sam Simone?" A voice called as I got out of my car.

"Yes, I am, but were not open yet." The man moved towards me.

"I don't want to go in the store. I need to talk to you."

"Okay, what can I do for you?" I asked in a hesitant voice.

"I'm a friend of your ex-wife I've been trying to get in touch with her."

"Well, it seems that you've wasted your time because I haven't seen my ex in over ten years. I have no idea where or what she's up to."

"That's weird, the way she used to speak about you, I would have thought that you knew exactly where she was. Are you sure?"

"I don't know who you are, but after she left, I spent years cleaning up her messes. I don't know where she is. As a matter of fact, I don't want to know. So, if you don't have anything else, I need to open the store."

"Nothing else, thank you. Watch yourself."

The man turned and climbed into his car. I went inside and started my day. I couldn't stop thinking about the man in the parking lot. Not once, had anyone showed up looking for Jane. The man's manner didn't fit him. He seemed to be playing a part. The last thing he said about watching myself had started the sirens going off in my head. It felt like a threat. I finished what I needed to do in the morning before heading to my office.

"Linda, hold my calls. I have an important call to make."

"Sure, Bossman, let me know when it's all clear." Linda went back to directing the store crew.

I checked my phone for messages. None seemed urgent, so I sat down to make my call.

"Mac, I had a strange visitor this morning in the parking lot at work."

"What do you mean by a strange visitor?"

"A man was waiting for me in the lot as I drove in. He was looking for Jane. He claimed to be an old friend. I told him that I hadn't seen her in over ten years and had no idea where she was. He thanked me and told me to be careful."

"Can you describe the man?"

"As much as I can remember, but it was a short talk. I'm not sure of my memory."

"I'll stop by after my meeting with Scooter. I may be able to help your memory. See you around noon."

"Noon is all right with me, thanks."

The store was busy, busier than on a big sale day. Sam stood watching as the customers shopped while employees refilled the shelves and helping answer the shopper's questions. The thought came to him that the store could go on with or without him. This seemed to sober him. He always knew it to be true, but when it struck him today, he filled with sadness. What would he do without the store and his job? The events of the past week weighed heavily on his mind. People that had played important roles in his life reappeared, only to leave again. Sam had no clue as to why. He would never understand Coben. Jane had been his whole world at one time, but time and distance made her just a person he once knew.

"Earth to Sam, we need you." Linda stood by him. He didn't know how long she had been there watching him.

"What do you need, Linda?" Sam felt like he'd just woken up from a long nap.

"Father Eugene and Andy are here with another man that I don't know."

"Are they in my office?"

"Yes sir." Linda headed back to the checkout stand.

Sam opened the door to his office. The three guests were sitting around the office talking quietly. "Sorry for the delay, it's just one of those mornings."

"Sam, let me introduce you to my replacement. Sam this is Father John Brody."

"Nice to meet you. I hope that your time here will be fulfilling." Sam shook the priest's hand.

"It is nice to meet you Sam, I've heard some very good things about you and the Good Samaritan Stores. My last parish didn't have a store. I'm hoping to become involved if the society wants me."

"I hope that you become involved with us too. The work is important. We meet the needs of a lot of people every year. Eugene, do we have time for a tour?"

"I think that we can squeeze it in. You do know that I'm leaving at the end of the month. I want John to see as much of the parish's activities as possible."

"Let's get started." The four began their tour. The first stop was the sorting room. Sam was glad to see the employees hopping. The first impression can make a big difference when the Society needed help from the parish.

"Wow, they look like they're really hustling. How many people work in this area?"

"Father, we have twelve in the sorting- pricing room. There are another six that handle donations and moving large items. Four employees work on the trucks. They do pickups and deliveries. That includes deliveries to our other two stores." Two employees are cashiers-store workers and we have three managers, plus a full-time person, mans the Society office." The group looked at the loading dock and the as-is yard before heading back to the store.

"What other programs do you have?"

"John, the store has a low- income senior job program, plus a community service section that Sam coordinates with the courts, and a high school job program for special needs students. Am I forgetting anything, Sam?"

"Just the appliance repair program that we use for the store and training some of the high school kids."

"I must say that I'm impressed. Sam it has been a pleasure meeting you. Eugene I will probably have a million questions, but I'll save them for later." The men exchanged pleasantries as the two priests left. Andy lingered behind.

"Andy, let's go into my office. You look like you have something on your mind."

"I'm not sure what I have on my mind, but something seemed a little off about our new pastor. He asked a lot of questions about all of the recent events involving you."

"How much do you know about him? Maybe he just likes mystery stories. I have too much going on right now to worry about our new pastor."

"Don't tell me, I watch the news. The killing at the soccer fields was played on all the channels. I thought that I recognized you and your cousin Mac in the background."

"I knew the victim. We didn't have the best background. Our reunion was short and nasty. Mac, lucky him, was the one that found him. And yes, I seem to be involved in too many of these things. It makes me wonder what I did in some past life to warrant all of this."

"Sam, I'm sure you were you in all of your past lives. Hang in there and watch yourself. I'll watch our new pastor. It might just be an old man's overactive imagination." Andy headed out. I sat down to ponder all of the strange occurrences of the last week.

There was a soft knock on my door around noon. Before I reached the door, it opened. Mac's hand was on the knob. "I just thought that I'd come in as quietly as possible. Do you have time for lunch?"

"Lunch sounds like a good idea. Any place in mind?"

"Yeah, *Rome's Best Pizza.* It's loud enough and crowded enough that no one will notice us."

"Let me tell Linda that I'm leaving for a while." I found Linda. Mac and I soon departed.

Paulo welcomed us with open arms. We ordered and found a table in back. The service is always prompt, so we were soon enjoying a Vatican Special. Mac and I didn't talk much while we ate, but once we had demolished the pizza we got down to business.

Mac placed a few photos on the table. I saw the man that had been waiting for me this morning.

"That's the man. Who is he?"

"That is Paul Layton. Sam you're lucky that he's not looking for you, but it seems that he wants Jane pretty bad. He must believe that she knows where Coben and Jones hid what they stole."

"Besides the photos, what came out of your meeting with Scooter?"

"Scooter is freaked. He knows that his life isn't worth much until Layton recovers the merchandise and cleans up the loose ends. He is worried that he's one of the loose ends. As for the stolen merchandise, it seems that the wrong stuff was taken. Our two dead friends read the serial numbers wrong and grabbed some really sensitive stuff. This wasn't discovered until Green Valley Technologies took possession of the delivery. Scooter said that his family went into emergency mode when they learned the truth of the screwup."

"Was Scooter able to give you any idea what was in the containers and how much he knew about Coben's plans to hold the merchandise?"

"He claims that he doesn't know what is in the containers. He said that Coben used a storage facility in the Valley near the Auburn Airport, but when he sent his people to get the stuff it wasn't there."

"Either Coben hid the stuff someplace else or Layton got there first and moved it, but I don't have a reason for Layton to move the stuff. Maybe, the double cross was in place all along. If we knew more about Layton and Scooter's family, we would have a clearer starting point."

"Scooter gave me some information on his family. I'd like Fatty to check them out." Mac gave the papers to Sam.

"I'll give these to Fatty along with some other areas that I want him to check out. We better get back to our regular jobs. Lunch is on me Cuz."

"Thank you, Sam." I paid the check and we headed back to Good Sam's.

DEEPER

The store was running smoothly when Mac dropped me off, so I made a dash for my office before anyone noticed me. I checked to see if Fatty was working off his community service hours. I was in luck, he was. I decided to go find him.

"Angela, have you seen Fatty?"

"Sure Sam, he's working on a project in the back. Do you want me to call him?"

"No thanks, I think that I'll go find him."

I headed to the warehouse area. We meaning, Linda, Bob, and I are making various changes in the store operations trying to improve our ability to handle donations quicker and more efficiently. The process is being implemented in stages. I'm not really sure what they were working on today.

At the back of the warehouse a number of employees are moving piles and marking areas to help streamline the handling of donations from the trucks or customers. For most of Good Sam's history, items were unloaded into big piles in the sorting area without any sense of what the items were. The changes should make it easier to sort merchandise after we have it, but the layout of the work area needed to be upgraded to speed things up.

"Well, look who's come to visit us mere mortals."

"Yes, I do need to mingle with great unwashed from time to time to reinforce my feelings of superiority."

"Bossman, you're so full of it. What do you need?"

"Just a short word with one of your minions."

"As long as you give him back, you can have him. Fatty, Sam would like a word with you."

"What's up Sam?"

"Let's take a break in the lunch room. It won't take long." Fatty and Sam went in the lunch room.

"I figured that you'd come and see me today. I have some more information for you and I'd bet that you have more for me to check."

"You're getting to know me pretty well. Maybe we should quit all of this and open a detective agency." Sam was laughing as he said this.

"Show me what you need and I'll give you what I've found." The two exchanged information. Sam only glanced at the new information. He would read it deeper in private. The file was fairly large.

"Anything that I should be looking for?"

"No, just a few surprises from your ex-wife."

"Thanks again, keep track of your time." Sam headed back to his office.

The file was very professionally put together. It didn't take long for Sam to find the surprises from his ex. It seems that she was involved with both sides of this mess. Layton and her had some type of a relationship. She, it seemed, was friendly with a couple of Scooter's family members, too. The report didn't show a direct connection with the crimes, but she knew more than she had told them. Sam locked the report in the safe and spent the rest of the day on store issues.

"Angela, I'll handle the till while you catch up on the store. That way everyone gets out of here on time."

"Sure Sam, I have to be home on time today, because I have company coming over."

"If you need more help with picking up the store let me know."

"I'm pretty sure that I can handle it." Angela started systematically cleaning up the store.

The last hour of the day can be really busy or slow. Today was a steady day. I didn't have too much trouble keeping up with the flow. About ten or fifteen minutes before closing I noticed that Mac walked in the door.

"May I speak with the manager, please."

"He's over at the checkout stand." Angela pointed towards me. I buzzed Linda. Both Linda and Mac arrived at the same time.

"Linda, can you watch the till? This customer has a complaint."

"Hi, Mac. Yes, I'll watch the till for you, Bossman."

"Hi, Linda." We went into my office.

"Have a seat. I want you to read Fatty's report." I opened the safe and retrieved the report. Mac silently read the report. When he finished. He looked up, "It seems that Jane hasn't told anyone the truth. She seems to be playing a very dangerous game. We might need to go talk to her again."

"I figured you'd say that. Fatty is looking into the stuff we talked about earlier. He should have something for us tomorrow." They sat quietly for a few moments.

"I can't go talk to her tonight. I have some work things to clean up. Maybe, tomorrow."

"I can't go tonight, either. Jude works late today. Let's shoot for tomorrow. We might have some more information to help get Jane to talk."

"Okay, tomorrow. I'll let you finish closing so you can get home."

The phone started ringing while we were closing. "I'll grab that, you guys finish closing. Hello, Good Samaritan Store, Sam speaking."

"Hey Sam, it's Fatty, I'm glad that I caught you. Do you have a minute?"

"Yes, but make it quick, I have to get David."

"I'll just give you an overview and e-mail the rest to you."

"That will work. What did you come up with?"

"I think that I found the person behind the double cross. Scooter's father and your ex-wife seem to have a relationship. I found e-mails and phone records between the two. This connection goes back at least five years. The stuff that I'm sending you will spell out all of this in detail. I believe that it will answer a lot of questions. When I get more info, I'll send it."

"Thanks, Fatty. I will call you if I have any further questions. I gotta go. Thanks again."

I grabbed my jacket and went out to help with the closing. The crew was pretty much done. It's nice to have an efficient staff.

"Were you peeking out the door to see if we were done?"

"Funny, Linda, very funny. The call was important. Did we have a good day?"

"About average for the beginning of the week. Get out of here. Give David a hug, okay?"

I didn't need to think twice about getting out of there. I jumped into my car and headed towards David's daycare. I had called Joey to tell him that I could get David after all.

David looked up and saw me by the door. My little whirlwind charged at me with the biggest, brightest, smile that I'd ever seen. He started telling me about his day. The only problem was that he was talking 100mph and everything came out at full volume.

"Slow down, little man, I can't understand a word you're saying."

"I'm just happy to see you Daddio. You don't come and get me very often, so I'm really happy to see you." He was hugging me with all of his might. I think my boy likes me.

"Well, get your things and maybe we'll get a treat on the way home." David set some type of land speed record grabbing all of his stuff. I barely had time to sign him out he was moving so fast. It has always been a special treat to know that your child or children like you.

It was an ice cream cone stop on the way home. We were very satisfied for a proud dad and a happy little boy.

The other kids were home when we pulled in the driveway. I headed to the kitchen to start dinner. Nothing fancy, a roast and some vegetables. Joey entertained his little brother and Marie set the table. There were some dishes in the sink so I washed them by hand, no sense running the dishwasher. By the time Jude pulled in the garage, the food was ready, the kitchen clean. My beautiful, but tired wife came in kissed me, smiled as she went to cleanup for dinner.

"I could get used to this, dinner, clean kitchen, and smiling faces." Jude looked wonderful as she came in and sat down at the table.

"I could get used to seeing your gorgeous smile, too!" I bent over and gave her a very good kiss, even if I say so myself.

"God, you two aren't together for two minutes without all these PDA's."

"What's the matter Joey, you're not getting any?"

"Dad, you don't ask people if they're not getting any. Now I'm not sure we can even eat after all this." We all started laughing as we sat down to a nice dinner, followed by a quiet night together.

KICKING BACK

"Why didn't you tell me about your plans for Rod and Coben?"

"The less, that you knew, was better for you and making our plans work. I hope that you can lead us to our merchandise. Your future depends on that."

"How can I do that? I told you that they didn't let me know their plans. You've known me for a long time, have I ever lied to you?"

"That is beside the point. Whatever we had changed when the chance for all this money came into play. Money trumps love." The call ended. Jane slumped over as if she had been stricken. The conversation had only made her plight worse. He would surely kill her when he found out that the merchandise was gone and she didn't know where it went.

Sam sat waiting for Mac to call him to let him know the plans. They were going to see Jane again after finding out her connection to Scooter's family. There had to be an answer in that connection. The phone rang. Sam picked up, "I'll get it."

Sam spoke into the receiver, "Hello, Mac, what's the plan?"

"I'll pick you up in a half hour. We'll talk about our plans on the way."

"Was that Mac?" Jude called from the kitchen.

"Yes, he said he'd be here in thirty minutes."

"Grab a sandwich. I don't need to remind you to be careful."

"No, you don't, but I'm glad that you do. Mac isn't one to take unnecessary chances. Hopefully, we won't be out there too long. But you never know when Jane is involved." Mac showed up just as Sam finished his sandwich. Sam gave Jude a quick peck on the cheek and headed out the door.

"Evening Cuz, I hope that you're ready to get some answers."

"That's kind of what I'm worried about. Jane is a loose cannon." They rode in silence. Nothing to hear but the road.

As Mac turned onto Green River Valley Rd. he turned to Sam, "It appears that Jane is in over her head. She has a connection to Scooter's family, but I can't figure the meaning of the connection. To tell you the truth, I don't trust Scooter. I think that he is using Tad and Tavin. I hate to believe that someone I've known all this time could be mixed up in all of this."

"My gut is sending me mixed signals. I can believe that Jane is in this mess, but I'm having trouble seeing what she adds to this. This wasn't just a setup to get revenge on Coben. They could have done a lot of things to get him. Something tells me that we need to find out more about the contract. Money is a huge enticement. Maybe, they're moving all the stumbling blocks out of the way. Do you know much about this other company or the history of the competition?"

"Hey, something just hit me. Where did Jane go to work right before your split-up?"

"I don't remember the name. It was a little machine shop in the valley. I think she was a receptionist. We split up right after she started there."

"It could be nothing or the link that we're looking for. Or I may be just throwing mud at the wall, hoping something sticks." The rest of the drive was quiet, both men, lost in their thoughts.

Mac turned off the road and started down the narrow driveway to Jimmie Mac's farm. As the car approached the house, Sam started feeling on edge. This feeling used to hit him every time Jane was in over her head.

"Mac, I think that something is wrong. Maybe we should park out of sight and work our way in."

"Okay, we'll put the car out of sight and see if everything looks normal. Stay behind me, I don't want to shoot you."

"I wouldn't want you to shoot me, either."

The two men got out. Sam followed Mac. There seemed to be a trail around the house. Mac motioned for Sam to move closer to the house. As Sam moved closer a shot broke the silence. A figure crashed out the front door. The figure had a gun.

"Stop, or I'll shoot." Mac had a steady aim on the figure. It was a man. The man turned attempting to fire his weapon. Mac calmly fired once. The fleeing man dropped and was still.

"Sam, check the house, I'll look after him."

Sam entered the house. He wasn't sure what he would find. Straight ahead he saw his ex-wife sitting against the wall. She was bleeding from a wound to her shoulder.

"Sam, you came to save me." Jane tried to stand up, but she fell. Sam caught her as he stepped towards her.

"Just stay there and we'll get some help for you. Is there anyone else here?"

"No just Layton. Did I hear more shooting?"

"Yes, Mac stopped Layton outside." Sam started putting some towels around Jane's wound to help slow down the bleeding.

"Sam, I'm coming in. How is Jane?"

"She has a bullet wound to her shoulder. Have you called in reinforcements?"

"They are on the way."

"Jane, can you answer some questions before the shit hits the fan?"

"I can, but I'm not sure that I will." Jane was still defiant.

"Why did Layton shoot you?"

"Because he was told to. Layton only did what he was told. He wanted the big payoff when the contract was awarded."

"Alright, who told him to kill you? Who's behind all of this?"

"Scooter." Jane passed out as she spoke. The sounds of sirens pierced the air. Mac went outside to greet the newcomers, Sam remained inside holding Jane.

The medics got out and Mac directed them inside. A detective approached Mac.

"Are you the person that called this in? Can I see some identification?"

"Yes. Here's my ID. The other victim is over there." Mac pointed at Layton's body by the driveway. The detective motioned another officer towards the body.

"You're Special Agent Delac?"

"Yes." Mac kept his responses short and to the point.

"Do you know the victims?"

"That is a man named Paul Layton and the wounded victim is Jane Jones. Officer I have a weapon."

"Okay, slowly remove the weapon and hand it to me." Mac gave the officer his weapon.

"The victim has a weapon that appears to have been fired recently."

"Special Agent Delac come with me." The two walked into the house. The room was busy with police and medical personnel working on Jane and the crime scene.

"Who is that?" The detective pointed at Sam still holding a now alert Jane.

"Sam Simone, we came together. When the shot rang out, Layton charged out the front door, Sam went inside to find Jane. I ordered Layton to stop, but he took aim at me. I fired hitting

Layton. This farm is my Grandfather's. Jane is Sam's ex-wife. Layton and Jane were involved in the killings last Sunday."

"Which killings?"

"Rick Coben and Rod Jones."

"Slow down, you've just given me information about two murders, and the shootings here. It seems that there are a huge number of gaps that need filling in." The detective moved towards Sam.

"I'm Detective Peters, King County Sheriff's Department. May I see your identification?" Sam handed his identification to the officer. Peters studied the it for a few moments.

"Your name seems to ring a bell. How are you connected to Special Agent Delac? The wounded woman is your ex-wife?"

"Mac is my cousin, Jane is my ex-wife, she was married to Rod Jones, and involved with Rick Coben. I'm not sure of her connection to Layton or Scooter Floyd."

"Who is Scooter Floyd?"

"Scooter is the CEO of Green Valley Technologies. This started with an accident and theft at the Cascade and Pacific railroad yard in Auburn. Green Valley Technologies was the victim of the theft. Mac went to Green Valley Technologies to follow up on the theft. Layton was an official for Green Valley. Mac and I coach a girls' soccer team. We played in a tournament at Alpac. The week of the tourney started with a series of odd events. My ex-wife came to see me for the first time in ten years.

She was in some type of trouble. It seems that her husband and lover were involved in some type of shady deal that had gone wrong. Her husband was Rod Jones. Her lover was Rick Coben. It also seems that she was involved with Scooter Floyd's family. Coben was also a soccer coach. We met again at the tournament. Our reunion was not very cordial. Witnesses will say it ended in a near brawl. When our teams played some of our former players showed up and taunted Coben."

"I know where I've heard your name. You've been involved with a number of cases over the last year or so. I'm going to go to the hospital to talk to your ex, so while the doctors are fixing her, I'd like to get a little more information out of you and Agent Delac."

Sam and Mac followed them to the hospital. The ride was very quiet. Mac found a space near the emergency room entrance. Sam picked up his cell-phone. Jude answered right away.

"Sam is everything okay?"

"No, that's why I called. We are at the hospital. Jane's been shot."

"Is she going to be all right?"

"I think so, but she'll be in surgery for a while. Mac and I are making statements to the police."

"Do you want me to come and sit with you? Should I tell the kids?"

"Yes, tell the kids, but don't come just to sit with me. I guess, do what you need to do for the kids. I love you."

"I love you, too! I'll say a prayer for Jane." Sam headed into the emergency room.

Sam soon found Mac. "Where's Detective Peters?"

"He's in with Jane. She woke up on the way to the hospital. I guess that she made a preliminary statement. The nurses are prepping her for surgery." The men sat in silence for a few minutes before Det. Peter's appeared.

"Good, you're both here. Ms. Jones made quite a statement. She seems to be scared out of her wits. I'm not sure that I blame her, but she got herself into this mess. Maybe you guys can give me a little more background on all of these people especially, Scooter Floyd."

"Scooter Floyd is the CEO of Green Valley Technologies. He also played soccer for both me and Rick Coben. Paul Layton worked for Green Valley. Coben and Jones are connected to Jane, Jones was her husband, Coben her lover. There seems to be an unknown connection between Scooter and Jane. We were going to see Jane and try to find out what the link is when we showed up at the property tonight."

"Agent Delac, can you give me any insight into how all this fits together?"

"I believe that there is more than one thing going on here. Scooter and Coben were involved in the death of one of our teammates around ten years ago. Buddy Johnson was killed in an auto accident in which both Coben and Scooter were involved. The accident still shows as active. We were waiting on some verification that Jane worked for Scooter or his family around the time her and Sam got divorced. The last thing is that Green Valley Technologies is competing with another company, I think their name is Puget Sound Industries, for a very lucrative government contract that will pretty much make the winner set for life, but I think that there's something funny about this, too. I came into this mess when we found that a shipment had been stolen while we were investigating a train car collision. It was a shipment for Green Valley."

"I'm sure that I will need to follow up on all this information. I will call on you when I can, plus we'll put security here for your ex-wife. I think that's all I need at this time." With a nod, detective Peters left the room.

"Sam, I think that there's more going on here. Did you have Fatty look into Puget Sound Industries?"

"It was on my list. He hasn't got back to me, yet. My feelings are twitching towards this being a set-up to eliminate some excess baggage. I don't want to believe it, but Scooter is the only one that has pushed the idea of revenge on Coben and his family turning on him."

"Scooter has always been a little outside the norm. I believe that Buddy's death still being listed as an open investigation is kind of odd. Add, that Jane may have been working for Scooter and that leaves a lot of things to be explained. Let's see if the nurses will let us talk to her." The nurse at the station flat out refused to allow either man to talk to Jane, reluctantly, Sam and Mac headed for home.

PART 5

A NEW DAWN

Mac rolled out of bed heading to his kitchen. Jimmie Mac was hard at work making breakfast. "Go take your shower. Breakfast will be done when you get out."

"Thanks, Gramps. I've got a long day ahead of me."

"Is Jane going to be okay?"

"Yes, from what information we could get out of the nurses. She is part of the reason my day is going to be long." Mac headed for the shower.

A few blocks over, Sam had started getting ready for his day. The house as always was a ball of confusion, everyone running around doing the Simone morning ballet. The amazing thing is that they all could get ready in time for their days.

"Sam, I'll pick up David after work. Are there any games or meetings today?"

"I checked everything twice, so I'm pretty sure that there is nothing on the calendar today."

"That's good. Call me if anything changes."

"I will. I've got to get going. Love all of you." Sam headed out the door.

"How is our patient this morning?"

"I'm not sure, the last thing that I remember was feeling this intense pain and I'm not sure if I was dreaming, but my ex-husband was holding me. He kept telling me that everything was going to be okay."

"You weren't dreaming, that was your ex. He may have saved your life. From what I understand he stayed until you were out of surgery. Sounds like a nice guy."

"He is. I just never realized that a guy like him didn't come along every day. It is just one of my long lists of stupid things that I've done to get here."

"Tim, it's so good to hear your voice. When are you coming home?"

"I'll be home on Thursday. A little birdy told me that Sam and Mac are in a predicament."

"That's a polite way of saying it. Sam's ex got shot last night. This is getting serious."

"How is she? How is Sam handling this?"

"Jane is going to survive. I'm not sure about Sam. Mac stopped by the bar after leaving the hospital. He didn't know much at that time. Mac shot the guy that shot Jane. He works for some Scooter guy that Sam coached and Mac played with. Hurry up and get home."

"I will. Love you."

"This is getting out of hand. Paul wasn't supposed to take things into his own hands. The sad thing is that we already have control of Pacific. If he'd just have waited it out, we would have all walked away with fortunes."

"This latest, might turn their focus onto more than just Coben's death. What are you going to do?"

"Pin much of the blame on a rogue employee. I believe that the paper trail is buried very deep."

"What about Sam, Mac, and Tavin?"

"What about them? They won't keep us from our goals. Sam has some notoriety as an amateur crimefighter, but he's in over his head this time. Just relax. Dream of your new life as a wealthy man. That's been our plan since Buddy had to go away. Chill out."

The chubby man hadn't slept for at least two days. He was focused on his computer. The stuff that Sam had given him was so compelling that he hadn't slept. He just followed the trail where ever it had gone. Everything was saved on a thumb drive. The overview he put in a folder. Fatty, exhausted, headed to his shower. He would need to get this information to Sam as soon as possible. Fatty was eager to see where this information would take the case.

By the time that Sam pulled into Good Samaritan's parking lot, Fatty, Mac, and Tavin were already waiting for him. "I can't say that I'm surprised to see all of you, but I'm glad that you're all here. Give me a few minutes to make sure that everything is running smoothly, before we move to the conference room for a little meeting. Fatty, lead them to the conference room, please. I'll try to be prompt. I know that everyone has places to go." The group followed Fatty into the employee area. Sam went into the store.

"Good morning, Linda, what is on the agenda this morning?"

"Nothing, Bossman. Just a regular day in paradise. Why do you ask?"

"I need to have a meeting with a few people. Things have changed since yesterday. Paul Layton shot Jane. Mac shot Paul Layton."

"Is Jane okay?"

"As far as I know she'll live, which is more than I can say about Layton."

"Layton's dead?"

"Yes, he died at the scene, while I was trying to stop Jane's bleeding. Needless to say, Mac and I had a very late night."

"We are going to have to get you a new hobby." Linda hugged Sam and kissed him on the forehead. "Don't go get shot. I don't know what I'd do without you." Linda had tears in her eyes.

The conference room was very quiet when Sam walked in. Each man lost in their own thoughts. Fatty had left his files and thumb drive at the head of the table. Sam took a few moments to read the synopsis of Fatty's information. Sam glanced around the table before he sat down.

"Mac, can you give a rundown on last night's events?"

"Sure, Sam." Mac proceeded giving a very accurate account of the shootings. Sam realized that Mac was a professional. It wasn't that he didn't know this, but it struck him that his cousin did this for a living. Maybe they had a chance to get to the truth.

"Tavin, please give us as much as you know about Scooter. Both, the company and his family connections."

"First off, I thought that I knew Scooter, but I have dug up some interesting facts since this started. There is also a bigger connection between Jane and Scooter. This goes back to the end of your marriage. Scooter has forced most of his family into giving up their power within the company. The family has no legal say in the company at this time."

"That's all in my report, too!" This started a heated conversation about all that the men had dug up.

"Everybody, settle down and we'll try to make some sense of all of this. First off, I don't believe that Layton was supposed to take out Jane. They knew where she was. I can't quite put my finger on what Layton's purpose was in taking out Jane, unless Jane's role is bigger than it appears to be."

"In my dealings with Layton, he always seemed to present himself as the most important person in the room. Scooter seemed to give him a lot of freedom when he gave him assignments."

"Tavin you need to give us as much information about your dealings with Scooter as you can."

"Well, Mac, I can only give you barebones information because I was Scooter's lawyer on many of these things, but I'll try to give you as much as I can." Tavin was becoming nervous about what would happen if any of this stuff got out.

"Sam, do you know much about the teacher?"

"Not really, Fatty, he played for me, but after the teams split, he stayed with Coben."

"I did some checking and it seems that he lived with Scooter's family for a time in high school. It seems that Buddy, Scooter, and Shipley got into a few scrapes along the way and that Coben stood up for the boys in court."

"This gets deeper every time we look. Tavin how about it. You stayed with them and stayed friends with them, what were they up to?"

"I'm kind of torn about all of this, Scooter's family helped pay my way through college. I owe them for the hand up they gave me, but they don't have any boundaries when it comes to money. The only reason that I didn't leave was that I would have left you guys holding the bag. They need to be stopped. But I couldn't do it alone."

"Now that Layton is dead, we won't know who or what will be doing the dirty work for Scooter. We need some answers. Fatty keep checking. Mac find out as much as you can through your resources. I'll talk to Jane if they'll let me. Keep your eyes open for any suspicious people. Make sure that someone else knows where you are and what you find." The guys got up to leave. Mac lingered to talk to Sam.

"Sam, I'll be by the house to ride with you to practice tonight. We can talk on the way, plus there is security in numbers."

"See you tonight, I hope that I can get something out of Jane." The men went their separate ways. Sam deciding to make an inspection of the warehouse. Nobody seemed to notice his presence until he entered the main sorting area. Sam watched as Bob placed his workers in the area that he wanted sorted first. The group began working through the merchandise. Linda and Bob had made a few changes in the way the donations were handled. Each sorter had helpers that moved the priced merchandise to the store or the areas for delivery to the other stores. Sam made a note to tell Linda and Bob that his first impression was favorable.

"Sam, how long have you been standing there?"

"Just a few minutes, but I can tell you that I'm impressed with the changes you guys have made."

"Thank you, I want to show you another change."

"Lead the way, Bob." The two men made their way to the back side of the warehouse. Right by the door to the loading dock was another pile of donations. This area used to hold overflow. When the inbound donations were coming in faster than the workers could keep up this area held the excess.

"See where the overflow used to be, that is now the double check pile. Everything is sorted again before discarding. We believe that the second set of eyes will recover enough usable merchandise to make it worth the cost."

"That's a wow. I think that I've seen enough. I'll say one thing, you and Linda are doing very good jobs. Your crews need to be celebrated, too! I'll let you know what we are going to do for the crew." Sam headed back to the store.

"If it isn't our long lost Bossman. As you can see, we have handled the load without you." Linda snickered as she said this.

"I have no doubts that you could easily handle the whole load without me. I have just witnessed what you and Bob have done in the warehouse. I must say that I'm amazed. The changes that you two put in deserve praise, so I'm going to put together an employee celebration for some time next week."

"You really like the new changes?"

"Very much. They add value while lowering costs. That's a winning situation in my book. I've already told Bob, so now it is your turn, good job."

"That means a lot, Sam. I have a few more ideas that I was waiting to talk to you about until after these changes worked or not."

"These changes seem to be working. Talk to me later this week about the new ideas. I have to leave at lunch today, but tomorrow should be okay."

"How's Jane?"

"That's where I'm going at lunch. I'll let you know when I come back."

THE WHOLE TRUTH

Sam pulled his car into the visitor's parking lot. It took him a few turns around the lot to find a space. He felt nervous walking into the main entrance. Something about Jane, always threw him off. The lobby was filled with visitors and hospital workers. A lot of people must be using their lunch hour to see patients or schedule appointments. Sam finally spotted the information desk.

"How may I help you, today?"

"I'm looking for Jane Jones."

"She is in Room 375. Go down that hall following the red line. The elevators are on the left. The room is on the third floor." The woman gave Sam a very pleasant smile as she pointed towards the red line. Sam thanked her and headed down the hall.

The elevator opened on the third floor. The nurses' station was right there. "Can you me tell if Jane Jones can have visitors?"

"Let me take a look, yes she can, the room is down at the end of the hall."

"Thank you."

As Sam headed towards Jane's room the nurse turned to her partner and commented, "I hope that he survives the visit. That woman is one unhappy human being."

From outside the door to Jane's room, Sam heard loud voices from inside. He couldn't quite make out the words, but he knew that tone from his years of living with Jane. Sam stepped into the room.

"Sam, oh my God, Sam. They tell me that you saved me. Come here." Sam hesitated before moving to his ex-wife. The nurse that was just having a very bad morning with Jane was astonished to see this transformation.

"How are you feeling? Have the doctors talked to you about your recovery?"

"I don't want to talk about that now. I want to thank you."

Sam leaned over and let Jane hug him. Jane started crying. After what seemed like an eternity, Jane let Sam go wiping away her tears.

"So, you're the famous Sam. I'm glad to meet you." The nurse extended her hand giving Sam a look of relief. She hurried out of the room. Sam sat down next to Jane's bed.

"Was I dreaming about Mac shooting Paul?"

"It wasn't a dream. We were coming out to check on you when we heard a shot. Layton charged out the door with a gun in his hand. Mac told him to drop the gun, but Layton aimed at Mac as Mac fired. I found you bleeding from your injury. You passed out while we were waiting for the police and emergency medical people."

"I know that I don't need to tell you about how many times that I've screwed up my life and the lives of the people around me, but this is the biggest one, yet."

"That's the second reason why we were coming to talk to you. This is becoming way more complicated than it looked at first. I need to know as much as you can tell me about Scooter. Everything points back at Scooter. From what we've found out, you've been involved with Scooter, Coben, Rod, Buddy, and the contract that Scooter's company is working on. That puts you right square in the middle of this mess."

"Sam, what would I know about all of these people? I've told you about Coben and Rod. What else would I know about this?"

"I know that you worked for Scooter starting around the time we split up. What is really troubling is that everyone in this, except for Layton, has ties to me. You can help me or you can take your chances. Just remember how well that's worked out for everyone going all the way back to Buddy."

"Sam, you can't be serious. Why do you thing that I have any knowledge about this?"

"Listen, Jane, you came to me to help you get out of this, but now you don't want to be straight with me. These people have been killing to protect themselves for over ten years. I think that you know more because you worked for Scooter. Plus, I know that a young rich guy paying attention to you adds up to more than just being a receptionist."

"I think that you need to leave. You've already convicted me without the facts."

"I'll leave, but think about your survival. I wouldn't be here if I didn't have the facts. I just want the holes filled in. Good bye Jane." Sam headed towards the exit. The conversation was puzzling at best. Jane was clearly holding back, but was it from fear or did she have another reason for holding back. The possibilities were rolling around his head as he rode the elevator. Layton or Scooter were intent on eliminating anyone involved.

"Excuse me, aren't you Sam Simone?" An attractive woman asked as Sam departed the elevator.

"Yes, can I help you?"

"You most certainly can. Do you have a moment? Maybe, we could talk in the cafeteria?"

"I have a few minutes before I have to get back to work." They walked across the lobby to the cafeteria. The woman ordered a coffee and Sam ordered a diet soda. There was an uneasy silence as they settled at a table.

"I know that you're wondering what it is that I want to talk to you about. I was just coming to see Jane and I believe that you were just leaving Jane."

"As a matter of fact, I was, but I don't see what I can help you with."

"Jane and I have been friends for a long time. I know a lot about you from our years of friendship, so I wasn't surprised to see you today. Jane told me that if she was ever in trouble, real trouble, that you were the one person that she wanted on her side."

"What is your name?"

"Cindy Floyd. I believe that you know my brother, Scooter."

"You're Scooter's sister? You do know that Scooter is responsible for Layton's attempt on Jane's life."

It took a moment before Cindy answered. "I'm not sure of that. How do you know that Layton was the shooter?"

"I was there when it happened. Mac shot Layton and I tried to keep Jane from bleeding to death. We've been looking into this since Rick Coben and Rod Jones were killed."

"Layton's dead?"

"Yes, the authorities haven't released all of the information. Your brother seems to be at the heart of all of this."

"I knew he was crazy. I just didn't realize how crazy he is. He removed the family from the company and made threats to stop anyone from going against him. I thought that Jane would be safe because of her relationship with Scooter. When you and Jane split up, Scooter was her boss. They had a relationship for a couple of years. Scooter broke it off for someone else. That's when Jane married Rod."

"This is news to me. I guess that I was too busy trying to keep it together for myself and my kids. So, you've known Jane from that time?"

"No, we were neighbors as kids. We lost touch for a few years. Then one day Jane applied for a job with our company. I walked into the lobby one morning. I recognized her at the front desk. We've been friends ever since."

"Well, Cindy, it has been nice meeting you, but I have to get back to work." Sam headed to his car with more information to sort out.

"Cindy, I'm so glad to see you. Come in and make yourself at home." Cindy leaned over and kissed Jane on the forehead.

"I was so scared when I heard the news. I've been praying for this nightmare to end, but Scooter is unstoppable in his thirst for power and money."

"I can't believe that he sent Layton to shoot me. From what I've been told, Sam and his cousin Mac stopped Layton, saving me."

"Well, honey, I just met your Sam in the lobby. He knows that Scooter is behind all of this. I got the impression that he and his friends won't stop till they bring Scooter in."

"That's why I told you that he was who I'd call in an emergency. Sam to rescue."

"I hope that one day when we're old we can look back and make a toast to Sam and his friends." Cindy was worried that Sam would dig up the whole truth, but that was a worry for another day.

EXPECTING THE WORST

The store had a steady stream of customers. Sam spent a good part of the afternoon helping at the front checkout stand. It was a relief to spend the day not thinking about murders, ex-wives, ex-players, and greedy business owners. Between customers and phone calls, Sam and the crew had to hustle to provide good service for everyone. Around four, the crowd started to thin out. Sam attempted to take care of some paperwork when he noticed a man lingering by his office. At first, he began feeling alarmed, but on a closer look he realized that it was Tim.

"Tim, how long have you been standing there?"

"Only a little bit, Hoss. I got in early from my tour, so I thought I'd check in and see what all the hubbub is."

"I don't know how much you've heard, but it is a big mess. Three murders and one ex-wife shot, along with a theft on Mac's turf, about sums it up. Also, the main suspect is one of my old players."

"Well, Hoss, after I go see my sweety, I'll get a hold of you and offer my services."

"Great, you know where to find me. I'm glad to see you, give Jody a hello from me."

Tim departed as quickly as he had arrived. Sam finished more reports before closing time. With the arrival of Tim, Sam was beginning to feel a little better about finding the truth. The more people that could follow leads and watch each other's backs would help them uncover the answer to this mess. The day ended without any more twists.

"Is that you Sam? I'm in the kitchen." Jude called out as Sam came into house.

"Yes, honey. Are the kids home?"

"Marie and David are here; Joey is at Ginger's house for dinner." Sam walked into the kitchen.

"The boy must be serious about Ginger. We have practice tonight. Mac is coming by to ride with us."

"Dinner is ready. Go get cleaned up. Please, call the kids." Sam gave Jude a hug and went off to wash up for dinner. As Sam walked down the hall, he called Marie and David.

"Daddio, you're home." David leaped into Sam's arms. Sam twirled the little ball of fire around. David squealed with delight. Marie came out of her room.

"How is that woman that gave birth to me?"

"She's going to live, but she hasn't learned anything from this mess."

"What do you mean?"

"I went to see her at lunch. She wasn't willing to give me any information on Scooter or his family. She is either stupid or scared, maybe both."

"She only believed other people before, so why would you think that she had changed now?"

"I don't know, but if someone tried to kill me, I would want to get them before they got me."

"See, that's the difference, you have a brain, she doesn't"

Dinner was a quiet affair. Everyone seemed lost in their thoughts. Sam didn't even notice when Mac showed up. "Earth to Sam, earth to Sam."

"Very funny Mac. I saw you there, but my mind is so busy rolling everything around that I didn't react."

"I know what you mean. I spent the day looking over all of our contracts with Green Valley to see if anything stood out, but everything seemed to just mix together making no sense at all."

"Mac do you want some dinner?" Jude asked.

"No thanks, I ate with Jimmie Mac."

"Marie, are you ready? We better get going. Don't want to be late. Jude be careful. We'll be back around eight."

"David and I will lock ourselves in. I plan to read some stories to him." Sam kissed Jude. They made their way to Sam's car and headed to practice. Nothing was said until they turned onto Valley Highway.

"Mac have you ever met Scooter's sister Cindy?"

"Scooter has a sister that's news to me."

"I met her coming out of the hospital today. It seems that she is friends with Jane. We talked a little before I had to go back to work. She filled in some of the holes. Scooter and Jane were a couple before Jane married Rod. My gut was screaming that they never completely ended, otherwise how did they all end up in this mess. Jane seemed to be afraid but defiant about her situation."

"Maybe, I can go at this from that angle."

"Cindy told me that Scooter forced the family out of the business. They or Cindy might want to do some pushing back at their rogue relative."

Sam turned into the field. Most of the team was already there. As they were getting the gear Sam turned to Mac, "Tomorrow you can start looking into that end. I'll check with Fatty and Tavin. Let's block it out and go play some soccer."

"Gather in everybody. I'll be quick. We have one week before our first league game. You guys looked pretty good at the tournament, even with the crappy end to it. Does anybody have any comments?"

"Coach I do." Suzie sounded very serious.

"Go ahead, Suzie."

"I agree that we looked good for this early, but we need to work on finishing. We should have scored more goals. We can't leave that many goals on the field."

"That's a nice observation. Mac and I have discussed working on finishing. One of my goals is to have every player score in a season. We came close last year. Keeping the pressure on the whole game will help us to finish. Does anyone else have a thought? Okay, let's get a good workout in."

The practice ended on a high note with a goal ending the scrimmage. The team was loud and happy as they left the field. "I have schedules. Grab one or two as you go. Pickup the gear. Practice Thursday at six."

Sam and Mac got into the car after every player had been picked up or left for home. Sam looked at Mac, as he pulled out of the parking lot. Mac asked about his meeting with Jane.

"You said earlier, that Jane wasn't willing to give you any information. Do you think that she is hiding what she knows or really is in the dark?"

"I think that she knows way more about Scooter and his plan, but is scared or trying to find a way to make a profit out of this mess. With both Rod and Rick gone, she doesn't have any hold over Scooter. I'm not sure whether she played the two sides off each other, but that is pretty much how she has always done it."

"What about Scooter's sister?"

"That's what I want you to check out. Find out all you can about her and the rest of the family. Jane and Cindy seemed to have been friends for a few years."

"Dad, can I ask you a question?"

"Sure, Marie, what do you want to know."

"Jane came to you for help and you guys saved her life, but now she won't help end this situation?"

"Yes, that's the story in a nutshell. Jane has spent her whole life doing what she pleased. After it ends in trouble, she expects the cavalry to come in and save her. I guess that I played that role for a long time, so it was only natural for her to come to me once more."

"Dad, it seems like she wants you to save her, but she has no regards for the pain it brings to you and all of us." Marie was looking out the side window as she spoke. Sam couldn't she her face, but he knew his daughter was hurting. The ride was quiet the rest of the way home.

Mac got into his car and headed towards Patty's house. The lights were on as he pulled into her driveway. Patty had a typical rambler. She had planted flowers all around her front yard. They were in full bloom shrouding the house in a blaze of color. Mac started up the walkway from the driveway to the door. The porch light came on as the door opened.

"Look what I found in my front yard." Patty laughed as she stepped towards Mac and gave him a friendly kiss, leaving him with a promise of more in the future.

"That is the best greeting, especially, after a long day. Do you greet everyone like that?" Patty smacked Mac on the shoulder. Mac gave her a big hug. The couple went inside and snuggled up on the couch.

"Can I ask you a question?"

"Sure Mac, what is it?" Patty had a worried look on her face. She felt very fragile with all of the crap that was going on around her. She didn't want to lose Mac before she got him.

"Do you know Cindy Floyd?"

"Sure, we go back a long way. We graduated together. I suppose we were friends at one point. Why do you ask?"

"Sam met Cindy as he was leaving Jane's room. Cindy wanted to talk to Sam before he left. It seems that Jane and Cindy were or are friends. Cindy said that Scooter has somehow taken over the family business, blocking them from access. We were wondering if you could give us some background on Cindy and the rest of the family."

"Is that why you came over to get information from me?"

"God no, I wanted to spend time with the most beautiful, intelligent, sexy woman that I've ever met." Patty stared open-mouthed at Mac. She wasn't sure if he was blowing smoke or he really meant it. Mac's look told her he meant it. Patty grabbed Mac and kissed him. It was a spectacular kiss. Mac felt the emotion shoot through him like an electric current.

"Man alive, I think that I just found the woman that I want to spend my life with."

"You better mean what you just said, because I feel the same way. Don't break my heart."

Marie went looking for Joey after she came in from practice. He was playing a video game in his room. Marie knocked on his door. "Can I come in?"

"Sure, what do you need?"

"I want you to drive me to the hospital." Joey gave Marie the strangest look. He was silent for moment.

"Are you sure that you want to do this?"

"Yes, I'm not asking you to go in, just the ride."

"I'm going in, she's my so-called mother, too!" Joey started putting his shoes on as Marie went to tell Sam and Jude that they were going out.

"Don't stay out too late, you have school tomorrow."

"Thanks, love you guys." Marie and Joey left in a hurry.

"What was that about?" Jude had a hunch, but she wondered if Sam was on the same wave-length.

"They're going to visit the prodigal mother. I think that Marie isn't happy with Jane's reluctance to help us after being shot by Scooter's henchman."

"Do you think that they'll be okay after seeing her?"

"That, I don't know. All I know is that we'll be here to help them land safely."

Marie and Joey were very quiet on the short ride to the hospital. The two were lost in the emotions of Jane's return and subsequent shooting. Jane had just been a thought that existed but didn't quite seem real. Them finally seeing her after all these years showed that she was real, but still an unknown to them. Children bounce back after a divorce, but many bits and pieces of them remained locked in dark places.

Joey stopped at the information counter, he got directions to Jane's room. The two headed for the elevators. The doors opened on floor three. Joey grabbed Marie's hand and headed towards their destiny. The door to Jane's room was open. Marie peered in hesitating before moving towards the figure in the bed. Jane opened her eyes to see her almost grown children standing in front of her.

"Oh my god, is it really you? Is your dad with you?"

"To answer your questions, yes, it is us, but no dad is not with us." Marie's tone was less than warm.

"Come a little closer. I'm not moving very well after being shot." Marie and Joey moved closer and sat down. There was an awkward pause as all three of them weren't sure of where to go next.

"I know that nothing I say can erase all of the misery I've caused in your lives, but let me tell you that I have wished there was a way that I could change what I am. I have plowed through my life creating messes everywhere I've been."

"That all may be true, but Marie and I didn't come to fix our relationship with a woman that never has been our mother. We came because you stirred up a hornet's nest. Putting all of us at risk, but you can't or won't help dad and Mac to fix the problem.

It's amazing that dad was willing to step up and help someone like you."

"You don't understand. They tried to kill me. How can Sam stop them? If I say anything, I'll be in worse trouble." Jane looked terrified.

"As usual, you've underestimated, Sam Simone. Dad will not back down. If he makes a promise, he keeps it. Come on Joey, let's get out of here."

"Wait, tell your dad to look into Cindy. He'll know what I'm talking about."

Marie and Joey came in through the garage door. Sam was sitting at kitchen table. Neither were surprised to see him. "How did your visit go?"

"It is hard to tell." Joey said as he and Marie sat down.

"Dad, we don't have anything to measure it against. She's a stranger. I know that I have no feelings about her, just an empty spot."

"Not much that I can add to that, but she did say for you to look into Cindy. She said that you would know what she meant."

"Are you guys okay?"

"Yeah, we'll survive. You gave us toughness. One thing I'll say, she is scared. I think that she's afraid to say more because they may try again."

"You might be right about them trying again, but we don't know the how and whys, yet. Both of you keep your eyes open for anything out of the ordinary. Good night. I love you."

Sam pulled into the store parking lot when he noticed a familiar figure standing by the door.

"Timothy, nice to see you so early in the morning. I thought you got lost when you didn't show up yesterday."

"Took longer than I figured to say hello to my sweetie." Tim had a large smirk on his face.

"Figures, let me open up. We can talk in my office." Sam disarmed the alarm, turned the lights on and made sure the heater was working. The two friends made their way to Sam's office.

"Most people would be in hiding or under their beds after all the shit been going on the last few weeks, but not you, no you're some type of old-time hero character."

"I'm no hero, but this shit as you say, is heading towards my family and people that I care for. There is no time to hide or cry for mama. I think that my team is better than their team. Nothing more, nothing less."

"That's my man. Give me some information and I'll give you my best." They talked for about twenty minutes before Tim got up to go.

"Let me know whatever you dig up. They don't know you, so maybe we can surprise them."

"Oh, we gonna surprise them. Once my guys start looking, they don't stop. Hey Hoss, I need to get out of here. Love ya, man." Tim disappeared as quickly as he appeared. Sam started feeling better about their chances of ending this mess. Mac, Fatty, Tavin, and Tim were all on the job, he'd take his chances with this team.

DOUBLE CROSS

The two old friends sat looking at each other trying to gauge what the other wanted. The mess that she had created could result in life changing circumstances. He had loved her at one time, but she had chosen family and money over a chance to get away and survive.

"Cindy, you have to find a way to end this before more people died. Many others will end up holding the bag for your fight with Scooter."

"I'm not going to let Scooter win again. He took Buddy away and made me choose his way or you. I can't change that, so I won't be the one that backs down this time."

"All of us that lived here paid a price for our involvement with your family. I lost you, but he still won't let me go. I want to live my life away from Scooter."

"If you help me, I'll do my best to help you live that life. I can feel the vultures circling around us. When this is done there may not be anything left for them to swoop down and devour."

"God, you're always so dramatic. I'll help you, but I need some type of assurance." Cindy looked at Tad and extended her hand. Tad reached out and followed Cindy.

Scooter paced in his office like a caged lion. He felt like the world was closing in on him. The plans he had made to pull off a bloodless coup had gone up in smoke with the three killings. The best that he could figure was that Layton had been playing both sides. The end result would be that both him and his sister were going away for a long time. That didn't sound like an appealing end to all of his hard work. His biggest blunder was allowing Coben and Jane to get caught in the crossfire. That opened the door for Sam Simone and his friends to get involved. Scooter knew that Sam wouldn't stop until his family and friends were safe. The news had been filled with his exploits over the last year, plus Scooter had personal knowledge of what type of man Sam is.

Mac was at his desk working on reports when someone knocked on his door.

"Come in, the doors open." Mac looked up to see Tim Tobegan walk through.

"Do you have a minute, Mac?"

"Sure, Tim, have a seat." Tim grabbed a chair and planted his self on it.

"I'll get right to the point. I have some information about a theft that happened in the railyard a while back." Tim handed Mac a file. Mac looked over the papers. Mac lowered the file and gave Tim a big smile.

"I didn't even know you were back. Sam got you on board pretty fast. I'll get a warrant and check this out. What else are you looking into?"

"I've sent some stuff to Fatty. If that plays out, I think that we should get with Sam and see if we can put an end to this shit." Tim stood up, gave Mac a nod and left. Mac sat still for a moment just drinking in all that was happening.

The phone rang in the empty office. The call was soon transferred to a cell phone. "I hope that this is important?"

"I think it is. We need to move the shipment. If by some miracle the stuff is found it will give them an easy route to us."

"Come on little brother are you getting antsy? You made the mistake of exposing us to Sam and Mac, so let me get us out of this mess. We agreed on putting all the blame on Coben and Layton. I've even come up with a way of taking care of the mystery of Buddy. You need to play your role and we'll end up being victims of double-crossing friends and employees."

"What about Jane?"

"Jane isn't going to be a problem. Layton's attempt on her life has scared the fight out of her."

"Okay, I'll follow your lead, but don't mess with me. We have enough on each other to give us state paid vacations for a long time."

"Hello is John there?"

"Just a minute I'll call him to the phone." The line went silent. It wasn't long before someone picked it up.

"This is Father John; how can I help you?"

"I know of a number of ways that you can help me, but today I'm only interested in one. Have you started to get Simone out of the way?"

"Yes, I have started, but these things take time. I should have the issue finished after the meeting tonight. It is usually a matter of having a vote for the records and I'll dismiss Mr. Simone as the dust settles."

"Just see that you do. We've made a large investment in you, so it is time for some return on that investment. Do you understand?"

"Completely. I'll finish the task that you've assigned me. When can we see each other?"

"Later this week. I hope that it is a happy reunion." The phone went dead. Cindy smiled as she contemplated her plan coming to an end.

A MEETING OF THE MINDS

"Hi, it's me. I'm just calling to remind you that I have a board meeting right after work."

"You'll be home about seven-thirty."

"That sounds about right. Don't wait dinner on me. I'll grab leftovers when I get home. I'll see you later. Love you." Sam went back to work. His mind wasn't on work or the meeting. He was still going over all of the stuff that had been happening over the last couple of weeks.

"Bossman, time to close it down." Linda was at his office door.

"I'll be right out." They closed out the day without too many problems.

"Sam, can I catch a ride to the board meeting?"

"Sure. You don't have the car today?"

"My mom needed to run some errands. She dropped me off this morning." The two headed out to Sam's vintage Thunderbird. Sam fired it up and they were overwhelmed with a blast from the stereo.

"Whoa, I must have been half asleep this morning. I hope that there is no brain damage."

"I wouldn't be worried about me; you drove all the way to work with it that loud. This crap seems to have you preoccupied."

"I admit that I'm racking my brain trying to figure out exactly who is behind this and why."

"You have a good crew working on the problem. Something is going to break your way pretty soon."

Sam turned into Blessed Family's parking lot and found a spot close to the entrance. Linda gave Sam a friendly squeeze as they went into the meeting room. The room was set up and about half of the expected participants were already there. Andy and Al were in deep conversation when they entered the room. Andy saw Sam and waved him over.

"Sam, Linda, nice to see you both. Sam, can I have a word with you?"

"Sure, let's talk over there." Sam pointed to the back corner. "What's on your mind?"

"I have had some more thoughts on our new pastor, I'm don't think that I can back him at this time for a spot on the board." Sam had never seen Andy so tense.

"Well, my first impression hasn't changed. I believe that there is an underlying issue concerning his behavior towards me."

"Al is with me on this, too!"

"Let's get the meeting started and see how it plays out."

"Everybody, let me have your attention, please." The people turned and waited for Andy to open the meeting. "Okay, take your seats and we'll get started."

The meeting started with the usual prayer and reading of old business. This took just a few moments. Sam noticed that Father Brody came in as the old business was being looked at. Father found a seat in the rear.

"That is all of the old business. I'll now turn the meeting over to Andy." Al sat down and Andy looked up taking the room in with a quick glance around.

"As most of you know, Father Eugene has been transferred. I would like to formally introduce you to Father John Brody. Stand up Father." Father Brody stood up and waved at the people in the room. Father seemed reluctant to do more than wave, but finally he started to speak.

"Thank you, Andy. It is nice to receive such a warm welcome from the Good Samaritan Society. I hope we have a long and harmonious relationship."

"Sam, can you give the store report?"

"Yes. The stores showed a 10% growth over the same month last year." A voice interrupted Sam at this point.

"I was under the impression that the Society was planning to hold a vote for my replacing Father Eugene. I don't understand why you've skipped that."

"Father, I don't know where you heard that we were planning to vote you on the board tonight or any time soon, but the officers have no plans to add you to the board at this time. I'm sorry if you misunderstood."

"You must as board members add me to the board. I'll not allow you to operate in my parish if I'm not added to the board. That is final."

"Father, for your information, you have no say in our operating in this parish. The rules clearly state that if an organization has operated in a parish for more than twenty-five years the pastor has no claim for membership or for removing the organization. Further, after your outburst we may never ask you to join us in any capacity. You are new to the parish and we had hoped to get to know you before deciding on the issue."

"You and Simone will regret making this decision. I'll be speaking to the Archbishop in the morning."

"Maybe this will keep you from making an extra phone call." Andy held up a paper for the priest.

"What is that?"

"A letter from the Archbishop explaining what his position is on this matter. As for your threat against Sam and I, bring it on. Good evening Father." Father grabbed the letter and stormed from the room. The Society members sat in stunned silence. Sam looked at Andy with admiring eyes. His old friend had stood up for him and carried the day.

"Thank you, once again for having my back. I'm even more convinced that Father Brody has an ulterior motive for coming to the parish. How did you get the Archbishop to intervene?"

"Well, I've known the Archbishop since he was called "Bugger". We have always kept in contact. He told me that some prominent donors pushed hard for Brody to replace Eugene. His Eminence is very interested in knowing the reason."

"Is everything in the letter true?"

"Yes, Sammy, all according to long established rules. I'd suggest that we all watch our backs for Brody's next move."

"Can you ask your friend who the donors are?"

"Al and I are working on it. We'll let you know as soon as we get the information."

After the meeting, phones lines lit up with news of the confrontation. The parish hadn't warmed up to the new priest, yet, but news of this strange event didn't help Brody's cause.

Sam walked in the door. The house was quiet. The quiet didn't last long as David spotted his dad and came a running. "Daddio, your home. I didn't hear your car. Are you trying to sneak in? Mom, dad's home."

"Sam, you need to call Eugene on his cell."

"Thanks, honey." Sam started to call Eugene.

"Hi, Sam, you got my message."

"I see the parish hotline is still working. What do you think?"

"You right about the hotline. I must have had forty calls. I don't remember Good Sam meetings ever having that many in attendance."

"You're right, only about a dozen actually witnessed the encounter. It wasn't pretty. That was one angry priest. I was kind of shocked when he singled me out. So, what do you know?"

"I don't know a lot, but somebody in or near the parish pushed hard for Brody to come to Blessed Family. The Archbishop is very curious and concerned about it, so he arranged for the change. I was fully briefed about the situation, but sworn to silence. In Brody's interview with the Archbishop he asked some strange questions about you. All I can tell you is to be careful and watch your back."

"Thanks, Eugene, I'd appreciate it if you can keep me informed. I'm beginning to believe that there is a connection between Brody and all the other stuff that is going on. Thanks, again and good night."

Sam could feel that there was a connection between Father Brody and the Floyd family. It almost seemed like they were muddying up the situation with so many different ways to look, that no-one would be able to find the right path in time to stop them. Time seemed to be playing a big part in all of this. The government contract had to be the reason for so many angles. Once the contract was awarded the Floyds would be set for life. Sam grabbed his phone.

"Fatty, this is Sam. I need you to look into a few more things."

"Sure Sam, what do you want me to check out."

"Can you see if the Floyds have any connection to Father Brody, Tad Shipley, and Tavin Long. See who has majority interest in the companies competing for the contract, also when it will be awarded. Let me know as soon as possible, okay?"

"I can already answer those questions. The Floyds paid for college and the seminary for all three, in fact, they adopted Brody and Shipley. Tavin turned down the adoption offer. The majority owners of both companies are Scooter and Cindy Floyd. The contract is supposed to be awarded at the end of June."

"Wow, I don't know what to say. How did you go down all of those paths?"

"Timothy gave me some information to track down. I just finished looking into it. I haven't called Tim back with the findings."

"Let him know. I'll call him later. Fatty, you are the best. Send me the bill."

"Don't worry about the bill, Tim paid it ahead of time. Talk to you later." Sam sat still trying to put the pieces together.

"Hey Mac, I hope it's not a bad time for me to call?"

"No, Sam, I'm just writing reports. What's up?"

"A couple of things, first off, I'm just checking to see that you're on for practice tonight."

"No problem, I'll come by and ride with you to practice. There are a few things I wanted to talk to you about our mutual friends."

"Well, that's was my second reason for calling. It seems that Fatty discovered some information linking the Floyds to both companies, plus Father Brody, Tad, and Tavin."

"I did find out that Scooter and Cindy bought the out their competition. How are the others connected?"

"The Floyds paid for college and the seminary, but the most interesting thing seems to be that the family adopted Brody and Tad, with Tavin turning them down. That may explain why Brody tried to remove me and Tad's interest in going to the tournament, but I'm not sure how it all ties together. My gut tells me that it goes all the way back to what happened to Buddy. Most of the individuals, alive and dead, played, coached, or were involved with someone from then."

"I got to go if I want to make it to practice." Mac signed off. Sam went into the kitchen to grab a diet cola and think. Joey came in with a smile on his face.

"You must have had a good day. You're grinning like the Cheshire cat."

"Just thinking about Ginger. Hey, Mr. Shipley asked about Marie's game this week. I told him that I'd let him know tomorrow."

"It's a home game at one. Are you going to bring your sweetie?"

"She's not my sweetie, but I think that a bunch of us are going to Lake Tapps."

"That sounds like more fun than a soccer game. Do you want a sandwich?"

"Sure, Dad, what type?"

"Tuna. Is Marie home?"

"Yeah, I think she's getting ready for practice. Thanks for the sandwich, Dad." Sam was all alone again. This was short lived, Mac knocked on the door and the house came to life as Sam opened the door.

"Come on in, do you want a sandwich or something to drink?"

"No thanks, my mom and dad came over and had dinner ready when I got home. Mom cooks dinner a couple nights a week when they know that I have practice."

"I know that no one has ever starved to death around your mom. I'm surprised that you and your dad don't weigh three hundred pounds."

"It takes some will power to not overeat when mom cooks. You're making me hungry just talking about my mom's cooking. I still don't eat Italian food at restaurants."

"I know, nothing is as good as your mom's cooking." Both, men started laughing. They had been saying this all of their lives. Family is one of the most important things in their lives which is why they were working so hard trying to find an answer to the murders and threats that were aimed at them.

Sam, Mac, and Marie were soon in the car heading towards practice. The ride was quietly short. Thoughts swirled through their heads. Soccer was the last thing they were worried about. Marie was still scrambling to figure out the re-appearance of Jane, Sam and Mac were trying to piece together the clues from the killings, but none of them had success coming to any conclusions. As the car pulled into the parking lot, each of them felt that soccer might let them step back from the issues.

Sam hopped out and saw a strange sight. Parents, more parents were at the field than usually showed up for games. "Dad, look at all the parents. We haven't seen some of them at a game for months, wow!"

"Did the Earth shift? I wonder what it all means? I guess we'll soon find out." Mac added.

"Well, let's grab the gear and go find out." The three of them headed towards the answer.

"Coach, Mac, nice to see you." Fred smiled as he greeted them.

"You too, Fred. Ladies grab the gear and start warming up." The team roared out on the field.

"I suppose that you're wondering why we showed up at a practice?" Jack Petty seemed to be the leader of the parents.

"Yeah, it had crossed my mind, but I knew that someone would get around to filling me in on the reason. So, what's on your minds?"

"We, the parents, wanted to let you know that we appreciate everything that you and Mac do for our kids. We also know that the events of the last few weeks have put a strain on both of you, so we are here to give you our positive support and reinforcement."

"I am flattered that all of you have taken the time to show us your support. I'm glad to see the turnout. As a coach and a parent, I welcome the support from all of you. It also gives back to each of your kids. Mac and I are hoping that we find a resolution to these events, but for now let's enjoy a little soccer. How about a parent-girls' scrimmage?"

The team was soon divided between the two coaches and any parent that wanted to play were added to the teams. For the next hour or so, a fun, but very competitive game played out on the field. Some of the parents were very good players. At the close of the scrimmage, all the participants were smiling and exhausted.

"I want to thank everyone for coming out tonight. This was a fun practice. Some of you parents might want to think about playing adult-rec soccer. Everyone be at the field at noon on Saturday."

"Thanks, coach, that was a nice way to get us ready for the league opener. I didn't know that so many of the parents could actually play."

"It surprised me, too, that so many of your parents could play, but maybe that's why you guys are so good. See you Saturday, Suzy."

Mac and Marie had already loaded the gear when Sam approached the car. Marie gave Sam a big hug. "What's that about?"

"Just saying I love you. That was a fun practice, especially after all the crap that has gone on the last few weeks. Seeing Jane, made me realize how much I love you. You never left us and you made us feel that we were going to be okay, but inside it must have been hard. I was too young to know how tough being with Jane had to be."

"It wasn't always hard, but Jane had a way of destroying everyone around her. I'm glad that you and Joey went to see her. That must have been hard, too!"

"Mac, see you on Saturday. You headed to see your sweetie?"

"As a matter of fact, I am. I'll call you if I get any more information about Scooter or his sister."

"Great, tell Patty I said hi."

"I will."

The morning announced itself with a great ball of fire from the east. One minute it was dark and the next it was a blazing mix of light pouring through Sam and Jude's window. No one could stay asleep with the brightness streaming through. Sam felt the warmth pour into his sore limbs as he climbed out of bed and headed for the shower. Stepping into the shower, it seemed that everything was pouring over him on this glorious morning. The water pouring over his body his mind was overwhelmed by a checklist of information about murder, betrayal, and fear. The blaze of the morning seemed to be helping him filter through all of these emotions and thoughts. By the end of his shower, Sam had a new resolve to combat anything that Scooter and his sister had to throw at him.

Sam was feeling completely restored as he ambled into the kitchen. Jude and David were making breakfast. This domestic scene always made Sam feel at peace. David didn't really make breakfast, but Jude let him think he did. Giving a quick prayer of thanks for his family, completed Sam's resurgence.

"David, what did you make for breakfast? I hope it's something good, because I'm starving."

"Of course, it's good, Daddio. Mom helped me with it. We've got eggs, sausage, potatoes, and toast. I buttered the toast just the way you like it." David excitedly pointed to all the food on the table. Sam was soon joined by the rest of the family. Nothing was left when they were finished.

"Thanks, David for that great feast. I think that I'll be full all day. I love all of you, but it is time to get on the road to work." All the Simone's left the house with smiles on their faces.

"Little brother, you need to get all of our cohorts together, so that we can discuss our plans for Saturday. I don't want any more screw ups."

"Don't let it worry your greedy little mind. Everyone will be at the house on Friday night to finalize the plans. We won't screw up this time."

"You better be sure, because I will not tolerate anything less than perfection."

Mac leaned over and gave Patty a kiss. Patty reached out and kissed Mac back. "Leaving already?" Patty pulled Mac down and gave him another kiss. The room started to heat up.

"I don't want to go, but I need my job. I'll pick you up Saturday for the game."

"I'll be ready. Have a nice day, Mac." Reluctantly, Patty loosened her grip on Mac. Mac was floating as he left Patty's house.

"Hey Fatty, it's Tim. I sent you some more info to check out. Bring as much as you can find to Sam's game on Saturday." Tim turned and looked at Jody. She was more beautiful every day. The baby had unleashed an aura around her.

"Chief, you're in early today. What's new?"

"I need to process some information. I need it by Friday night."

"Let me see what you need, maybe I can help you."

"That would be great, Steve. Here is the stuff that I need processed. Anything that you find will be good." Officer Sebastian took the folder and went to his desk to start his search.

"This is Eugene. Yes, Bishop, I would be glad to do you a favor."

"Eugene, I want you to go to this soccer game on Saturday. Sources tell me that it is important for us to be there."

"I'll be glad to attend the game. Sam's teams always put on a good show. Is my successor going to be there?"

"That is what I've been told. It seems that everything is heating up. Be careful, and let me know the details." The call ended on that note.

The old Thunderbird pulled into the Good Samaritan parking lot. Sam headed to the entrance. The morning was sunny and cloudless, not a hint of the usual rain in the air. Linda's car was the only one in the lot. The start of a new day put a smile on his face as he entered the store. Sam saw Linda picking up the store. He stood watching her work. It was a sight he seen hundreds of times before, but this morning it made him realize how much he cared about Linda. He watched for a few moments before Linda became aware of him.

"How long have you been watching me?"

"For a while. I can't tell you how much that I love mornings like this. You have been a constant in my life for a long time. You, me, and this store."

"I like you too, Bossman." Linda didn't say anymore, but her long suppressed feelings were howling around her. She wouldn't trade their friendship for anything.

"Are you ready for the manager's meeting?"

"Bossman, I was born ready. Just show up at ten in the Employee room. Everyone is supposed to be there."

"That's good, because I plan to give a few atta boys to the crew. The stores have been performing way above their goals and expectations, especially this store."

"Thank you. I work really hard to meet the goals." Linda was beaming with the news of the store's performance. Sam only handed out compliments when they were earned.

"Well, keep up the good work. If I haven't said it before I'll say it now, you are the best." With that, Sam turned and headed to his office.

"Mrs. Tobegan, we are going to a soccer game on Saturday. I need to be there to watch Sam's and Mac's backs."

"Is all of this crap coming to a head?"

"Sam seems to think so. I'm pretty sure that he is right. I'm hoping to keep things from getting out of hand. Maybe, you can sit with Jude and keep an eye on her and David."

"I don't want anything to happen to my pregnant Queen, but I may need you to be our getaway driver."

"Sure thing, Rock Star, I'll sit with Jude and talk about kids. You just try to not get hurt or in trouble. I don't want to move to Walla Walla to see you."

"Give me a kiss Mrs. Rock Star." The two kissed as the scene faded to black.

Sam was busy with the usual paperwork and messages when he realized that it was time to head to the manager's meeting. "Angela, I'll be in the employee lounge for the manager's meeting. If it is really important call me, otherwise I'll take care of it when the meeting is over."

"Sure Sam, I'll handle anything that I can." Angela went back to the line of people at the counter. Sam knew that she would do the best that she could. The store was crowded as he weaved among the shoppers heading towards the Sorting room. Sam greeted or acknowledged people as he went.

The managers were all inside the room when he entered. Linda waved him towards her. Linda was talking to Denise from Four Corners. "Sam, Denise and I have been discussing ideas to help promote the stores, they sound terrific."

"Hi Denise, I'd love to hear about your ideas at the meeting. Anything that promotes the stores is a good thing. Linda, I need a moment before we get this meeting started."

"Sure, Sam, let me know when you're ready." Denise and Linda headed to their places as Sam pulled his phone out to check his messages. Fatty had sent him a message confirming what he had dug up from Timothy's request. Sam smiled as he read the text. After reading the text, Sam's mood improved immensely. With a nod from Sam, Linda opened the meeting.

"Thank you all for coming. Let's start with a prayer." Linda led the group in reciting the 'Our Father.'

"Everyone, pick up the emergency instructions in front of you." A quick review of exits, fire extinguishers, and closest phones followed. A safety leader was chosen from among the attendees. Finally, the meeting was ready to cover the topics.

Sam stood up and began delivering his monthly report. "It is a pleasure to go over this month's report. The stores all had excellent months. Every goal was met or exceeded. There were no major negatives in service or community support. That means my phone didn't ring off the hook with complaints. You and your people did their jobs and did them well. The stores have had a five-month run of exceptional sales, profits, and just damn fine work. The board and I want all of you to know that we really appreciate all of your efforts. Each manager will receive a bonus for your efforts. Each employee will be getting a fifty-dollar gift card, too! Once again, I'd like to say thanks." Sam sat down. There was an eerie silence, but the room soon exploded in happy applause. The rest of the meeting went by pretty fast. Some new ideas were introduced and tossed around the group. Nothing was decided, but the meeting ended on an upbeat.

"Marie, is it true that Jane came back and got shot?"

"Yes, I wasn't going to talk about it because she really didn't come back to see me and Joey."

"I'm sorry, how is she? Have you seen her?"

"Don't be sorry, Suzie, you've always been there for me, not like Jane. Jane is somehow involved with the coach guy that got killed. I don't know or want to know all of the dreary details, but these creeps tried to kill her, Mac and Dad showed up and saved her."

"Your Dad is an amazing dude. The most exciting thing my Dad does is going to work every day."

"Suzie, you have a great Dad. He's funny and nice. I would trade that for all of the weird stuff that has gone on around my Dad for the last year."

"I know. I love my Dad, but yours is like living in a reality show. Did you go see your mom?"

"Yeah, Joey and I went a couple of nights ago. It was very hard to talk to this stranger. We have nothing in common with her, except our births. The strangest thing is that she came to my Dad when she got in trouble because she knew that he would help save her. That's messed up."

"Are you ready for the game Saturday?"

"I was born ready." Both girls burst into the giggles as they hugged each other.

"Chief, I have the information that you asked for."

"Thanks, Sebastion. I hope it gives me some answers." Chief Petty went into his office. The information revealed more about the Floyd family's business practices. Petty made a phone call.

"Special Agent Delac, how can I help you?"

"Mac, this is Jack Petty. I have more information on the Floyds."

"Great, Chief, everything we learn brings us closer to ending this."

"Maybe we can get together to look at all of our notes. I believe that the game on Saturday is really important to this mess."

"Let me talk to Sam. We might want to get together at The Big A. Jody will let us use the back room. I'll call you back."

"I'll wait for your call." The call ended. Mac started calling all the parties.

Sam was taking a walk around the store's grounds when he saw Fatty. Fatty looked up and waved Sam over.

"Just the man that I was looking for. Fatty, can you make it to The Big A tonight around six?"

"Sure Sam, what's the occasion?"

"We all need to get together and look at all of the information we've gathered about the Floyds."

"I'll be there." Sam continued on his walk.

"Jude, I'll be a little late from work. I have a meeting right after work. Not sure how long it will take, I love you." Sam ended the call after leaving his message.

GAME TIME

The Store was overflowing with customers. Sam hadn't had time for a break in nearly two hours. Linda, Angela were hopping just as fast as Sam, but there didn't seem to be an end. Bob's backroom crew were just as busy. They unloaded an endless stream of donations. It was a beautiful day which must have made everyone within miles get out to shop and enjoy the weather. Sam was loading some furniture into a van when he realized that the parking lot was almost empty. With a sigh of relief, Sam headed back into the store.

"Hey, Bossman, I think we've crested the wave. What a rush. This looks like it will be a good day."

"It seemed like there'd never be an end to that throng. You guys, all of you did a fantastic job. If you don't need me anymore, I think that I'll catch up on some stuff before the weekend."

"You have plans for the weekend?"

"Just our first game of the season. Other than that, nothing special."

"Tell Marie, good luck."

"I will. I hope that you have a good weekend, too!"

"That's a laugh. Cleaning house and laundry are not my idea of a good weekend, but maybe something better will come along and change my destiny." The two laughed as they walked to their cars.

Sam scanned the parking lot as he pulled into The Big A. It was early on a Friday, not many cars were in the lot. The place never seemed to change. Memories flooded Sam's head as he walked through the door. The bar was subdued. The music was low. Most of the patrons quietly sipped their beverages lost in their own worlds. Jody spotted Sam as he moved through the bar.

"Over here, Sam." Sam acknowledged Jody, as he headed towards her.

"Hi Jody, is anyone else here?" The friends hugged.

"Mac and Tim are in the backroom. I'll direct everyone else there, as they arrive."

"Thanks, Jody." Sam made his way through the small crowd. He only saw a handful of people that he knew.

"Have a seat, Sam. I ordered you a diet cola. Hopefully, the rest of the guys show up soon."

"Thanks, Mac. We'll get started when they arrive." The men spent a few moments watching the interactions among the bar crowd. They were very relaxed with each other. All three had known each other almost all their lives.

"This is one lame party." Tavin exclaimed as he and Fatty walked in, soon followed by Jack Petty. Father Eugene was last to show up. Father's appearance seemed to surprise Sam.

"Eugene, it's a pleasure and a surprise to see you."

"Well, Sam, my boss seemed to think that it was a good idea for me to watch over this weekends game. I called your house, Jude told me where you were, so here I am."

The group made small talk as the refreshments were brought.

"I think that we should share all of the information that's been gathered. Take a few minutes to look over the info. Afterwards, we'll talk about what we know. We can give input as to how we can use it." Sam handed out his files. Everyone exchanged what they had dug up. The men poured over the information before Jack Petty spoke up.

"I have sent most of this information to the other jurisdictions. I believe that we have enough for warrants for Scooter, his sister, the teacher, and the priest. I'm sure that there will be a confrontation at or after the game on Saturday. All of the departments will be in attendance at the game."

"Jack, I feel the same about the game. We need a plan to keep the girls and families out of harm's way. Maybe, if we catch them by surprise it won't turn ugly."

"Sam, that's why I've set this in motion. If all of us can keep tabs on Scooter and his friends we'll bring them down without too much mayhem."

"Chief, they don't know me, so I should be able watch them once they show up."

"Timmy, I'll get with you to work out how we need to communicate during the game."

"Tavin don't act out of the ordinary. You know them better than any of us, so just be yourself." The group went over a few more things before it broke up. Mac and Sam walked Tim and Jack out to their cars.

"Jack, I won't ask for anymore details. I just want to make sure we keep the innocent people out of the way."

"That's what I've been praying for all day."

"You're a good man, Jack Petty."

"Eugene, how much of this did you and your boss know before the meeting?"

"Enough to realize that it would involve the diocese pretty deeply. The Boss wants to see an end to his rogue priest, before it gets worse. One thing that I can tell you is that I will become the new old priest at Blessed Family." Eugene gave his friend a hug and a smile.

"That's great news. Welcome back. I might even have to make it to Mass once in a while."

"I think that it may be a sin to lie to a priest." The men laughed.

The Simone's spent a quiet evening each lost in their own thoughts. Sam couldn't escape a feeling of dread over the conclusion that he expected in the morning. It wasn't a Will Kane sense of duty, but a sense of not knowing if the problem would be solved. He didn't want any of these good people getting hurt or worse. He had seen enough people hurt since this started. The why of how he was pulled into this mess still escaped him.

Jude and the kids were praying that nothing would happen. Marie and Joey wanted everything to go back to normal. They wanted Jane to go away. It seemed that her appearance just added to the inner misery they had suffered. Jude didn't want Sam to be a target for so-many people. She knew that if her husband could help, that he would step into harm's way to do it. Sometimes it was scary to be married to Sam.

Mac and Patty spent the evening holding each other. They hoped that the day would bring some closure to Patty about what really happened to Buddy. Both, felt that the only positive of this was that they were now together.

Jack Petty was up early. He spent the time making sure that his department and the other jurisdictions were on the same page for the day's activities. Once he felt convinced that everyone knew their parts, he was able to breathe a sigh of relief. Teamwork was as important in police work as in soccer.

Sam rolled out of bed, still weary, but resigned to the day ahead of him. He could hear the sounds of his family beginning their day. The aroma of food wafted through the house. Following the smell, Sam headed to the kitchen.

"Daddio, you're up. Come see what we're making." The little boy smiled and bounced as he beckoned his father over.

"Wow! A feast fit for a king. Can I have some?"

"Don't be silly. Mom says we have to feed you."

"You have to feed me, I'm insulted. I'm tempted to just not eat a thing, but it smells so good, and you went to all the trouble to make it. I guess that I'll have some."

"Watch it, Buster, you might just get your wish." Jude's reply sent David into peels of laughter. My family is so funny. It as if a real funny guy, like me, can't even get a good joke in. The Simone's were soon all gathered round eating breakfast and enjoying their time together. The day's problems pushed back for a few moments.

"Joey, I know that you have plans today, but please keep your phone on and near you. I'm not saying that anything is going to happen, but in case we need you, have your phone ready."

"Sure dad. We're going to lake Tapps. If you need anything I'll be there."

"You're a good boy "Charlie Brown".

"Marie, if anything happens at the game, you are to get your teammates and head to safer ground. Maybe, behind the concession stand."

"I can do that. Are you sure that this is going to come to a head today?"

"No, but I'd rather be prepared than not ready. Jude, Tim and Jody will help you with David."

"Sam, I know that I've said it before, but you better be careful. If anything happens to you." Jude let the sentence just hang there.

"How are you today? I hope that things are getting better?"

"Most of me feels better, but it is still pretty sore around the wound. I was able to get up and walk last night. That felt okay, but it sure tired me out." The phone rang while they were talking.

"Yes, she's right here." The nurse handed the phone to Jane.

"Jane, get out while you can. All of this is going blow up today." The line went dead.

"When is my doctor coming by?"

"He's in surgery now. I would think by lunch."

"Thank you." Jane waited until the nurse had left to start dressing. She wasn't sure where she was going, but she was going. The warning call had spooked her. Jane hadn't been involved in the mess, so she wasn't planning to be one of the fall guys. She had seen how Scooter and Cindy had cleaned up their messes before. They had tried to kill her. That wasn't going to happen again.

Back in her clothes, Jane was able to walk to the elevators without being detected. Outside the hospital, Jane quietly waited for the cab she had called. The cab pulled up and Jane disappeared.

The hastily put together task force went over the details of the raid that was planned for this morning. King County was the agency in charge. Auburn, Twin Rivers, and Alpac were assisting the county. They would serve a search warrant at the property. Arrest warrants had been issued for at least three of the individuals involved. The Floyd family compound was under surveillance since yesterday. The group would soon arrive at the scene before serving the warrants.

"Scooter, try not to screw it up this time. We have too much at stake. I can't believe that you couldn't take care of your old coach, Jesus, it's as if you think that he can walk on water." Cindy hadn't let up on her brother for days. The others in the room didn't say anything to defend Scooter. They knew better. Cindy's wrath could scorch the earth.

"Where is Tavin?" Father Brody looked around the room like a condemned man.

"I think that our one-time friend has chosen his team."

"Shut up Tad. You are such an idiot sometimes."

"Well, I'm not the idiot that got us into this mess." Tad stared at Scooter and Cindy.

"Nothing ever stopped you from taking our money and help, just shut up."

"Cindy, we won't fail, so relax."

"When the job is done; I'll relax. Anyway, it is time for you guys to get on the road."

The three men headed out to Scooter's SUV. The rig was already loaded with whatever they thought was needed to put an end to the situation. As soon as the vehicle turned at the intersection. The task force made a final check and gave the signal to proceed. The house was soon surrounded. Carefully, the group approached the door.

Sam pulled his car into the stall next to Mac. It was a gorgeous morning, just about a perfect day for soccer. If the outside problems weren't hanging over everyone's heads it would be; perfect. The small group moved towards the field. They collected more players and parents as they approached the sideline.

"Mac, I see a few of our friends in the park. I hope that we can avoid serious problems."

"Look at the far parking lot. The unwanted guests have arrived." Mac pointed at Scooter and company getting out of their cars in the back of the parking lot.

"Well, it seems that whatever they have up their sleeves is going to happen. We've got a game to play, so let's start our warm-ups." Mac looked at his cousin. He wasn't sure about Sam's reaction, but he was right they had a game to play.

Behind the restrooms and concession stand Chief Petty was meeting with a few of his officers, all in plain clothes, Fatty, Tavin Long, Father Eugene, and Timothy. Timothy had a few of his associates already placed around the field.

"Everyone, listen up. Do not approach any of the suspects. Watch and report. Just be careful. I'll be watching the game like

I would normally. Any questions?" No one spoke up. The men were soon spread out along the field. To most people it looked like they were there for the game.

Sam and Mac tried to run the pregame workout like any game, but it was hard to concentrate on the field when there were distractions all around them. The referee came over for the pregame inspection. The team gathered round.

"Sam, your team looks good as always, so I'll call for captains in about five minutes."

"Marie and Petty, you're todays captains. Take the west goal. Anyone that needs to use the restrooms, do it now. Suzie, call out the lineup." The girls all had little rituals that they did before games. The team looked ready. Sam felt a twitch in his stomach. The twitch was more about Scooter and his guys, plus the assorted police stretched out around the field.

Cindy was making a latte when she heard noise at the door. Jesus, how could those guys have screwed up so soon? She was a little mad as she made her way to the door. As she opened the door, she started to berate her brother, but it wasn't Scooter.

"Police, we have a warrant." All Cindy could see was a large group of police at her door. She started to slam the door and run. The officers had her on the ground in seconds. Cindy stopped fighting the officers. She was soon cuffed and moved to a chair. The house swirled with activity as the officers searched for evidence. Cindy knew that it was all over for her. Survival mode kicked in as she felt her life as she knew it ending. The fear of being caught and sent to prison had chased her since Buddy was killed. She made a decision to turn evidence against Scooter and her adopted brothers.

SOCCER-TIME

Sam felt a sense of relief as the game started. Nothing had happened, so he hoped to be able to concentrate on the game. The Roadrunners started out looking like champs. They kept the pressure on their opponents. Suzie sent a pass through a gap that Marie flicked into the corner of the goal past the outstretched arms of the keeper. This held up to half-time.

"Nice half, but we aren't creating enough chances for the offense. Is anyone hurt?" No one answered, so Sam and Mac talked about the adjustments they needed to make.

"Put more pressure on them. We aren't going to get any cheap goals. Defense play tighter. Talk and hustle. Everyone in." The team gathered around Mac. Sam stepped in.

"I just want to tell all of you to have some fun. Now go get them." The girls ran on to the field.

As the second half started, a man approaches the sideline. He stopped next to Chief Petty.

"Chief, we have the subjects pretty much boxed in. They haven't done anything out of the ordinary, so far. I've also received a message from the county. They have served the warrant and taken one suspect into custody. The suspect is co-operating with them. They will be here for the other suspects as planned."

"That's good news. Let me know if anything changes." The man disappeared into the crowd.

"Well, Ms. Floyd, I'll see what we can do since you've been so accommodating."

"I'm not going down because my brother and his friends are so stupid. I have evidence on a few earlier crimes, too!" The commander nodded to the deputy to take Cindy away.

"That is, one messed up person. She is clearly the brains behind all of this. She just sold all of her family down the river. That's sick." The commander gathered his squad to leave for the soccer game.

"Scooter, I have a bad feeling about all of this. It seems like we're being squeezed."

"Christ, Tad, man up. We've planned this out. If we follow our plan, nothing will go wrong. This is family business. All we want to do is get Sam to get out of our business."

"It is more than Sam. It's Mac, that police chief, and Sam's rocker friend. They are very loyal and we can't be sure that they'll stop after Paul shot Jane. It seems that even Tavin is on their side."

"Relax, have you ever seen Cindy's plans fail?"

"There is always a first time."

A figure approached Father Brody. Brody didn't see him until he was right next to him. "I see that you're still doing the bishop's scut work."

"You might call it scut work, but I'm just doing a favor for my boss. You might remember that he is your boss, too!" The two priests stood quietly staring at each other. Both men knew that the day was going to end badly for one of them.

"It may be hard for you to understand, but this my family. They helped me when my parents died. I couldn't have become a priest without their help."

"That may be true, Father, but what type of a priest are you? I think that's why we're standing here today."

"Get away from me you sanctimonious jerk." Father Eugene stepped away.

The second half of the game was turning out to be a hard fought, well played battle. Neither team could find an advantage. Sam and Mac moved players in and out of the game trying to gain an advantage.

With a little over ten minutes left in the game the Roadrunners defense had a costly slip. Petty fell while guarding her opponent. This left the girl wide open for a pass which she sent into the corner of the net. Game tied. The teams pushed hard for the last minutes, but regulation time ended as the Roadrunners sailed a shot over the bar. The game would go to overtime.

OVERTIME

"Everybody, gather in. We have ten minutes to pull this out. Push hard. Captains, we want the ball. Same lineup that ended the game. The rest of you be ready. Mac, do you have anything to add?"

"Defenders, clamp down, don't give any ground. Clear or knock the ball out if you can't lose your support. Just keep doing what you've been doing." The captains came back.

"Our kick, we defend the east goal."

"Great, remember, put pressure on them. Don't let up." With a roar, the team sprinted onto the field.

The Roadrunner's put on an impressive display. They kept possession of the ball for almost the whole overtime period. The girls pounded shot after shot at the goal, but the other team played with a fury defending that goal. As the period wound down, Marie sent one last shot just over the bar. The whistle exclaimed the end of the overtime period. Tired players retreated to each side of the field.

"It's time to make our way towards Sam's car. Does everyone know what they need to do?"

"Sure, Scooter, we'll be ready when they show up." As this little meeting ended, another group arrived at the entrance to the park.

"Let Chief Petty know that we are here and ready to deploy. Move into position. I'll give the order to move in when we are ready." The officers quietly left their vehicles to move into position.

"The Chief has been notified. His men are dispersed around the park."

"Do we have the suspects in sight?"

"Yes, the ones we have warrants for are in a group near the far side of the soccer field. I understand that there are some hired help in the area."

"Let's see if we can intercept these private security guys."

"I'll see if the Chief's men can identify and surround them."

"Good job, I'm going to get closer to the field. I like soccer." The commander smiled as he moved towards the field.

"Listen up, this is the shootout lineup. Petty, Suzie, Linda, Nancy and Marie in that order."

"Coach, I've never been in a shootout. I'm kind of nervous."

"Suzie, you'll be fine. You've taken penalty kicks in games and practice. Relax. The world won't end if you miss."

"I don't want to let my teammates down."

"You couldn't let down anyone if you tried. Anyway, I'll still like you."

"Thanks, coach." Suzie smiled as she went to join her teammates. Sam announced the second five in case the shootout ended in a tie. The first five from each team went out to meet the refs and get instructions for the penalty kicks. The girls were lined up in order on both sides of the box. The Roadrunners won the toss and elected to let their opponents shoot first.

"Sam, I have a good feeling about the shootout. Remember when we beat Coben's team in penalty kicks?"

"I was just thinking about that. Coben was still yelling as we were getting into our cars."

The sidelines got deathly quiet as the first shooter stepped up. The girl quickly punched a shot into the corner. No chance to save that shot. Petty confidently placed her ball on the spot. She looked up and drilled the ball into the net. 1-1. A small girl eagerly stepped up and with little wasted motion sent the ball into the top corner. Suzie was next. This looked like a different Suzie. This Suzie put the ball on the spot and faked the keeper one way as she tapped the ball the other way. 2-2. The girls mobbed Suzie after her shot.

"Mac, this is going to come down to the last kick. I hope Marie is ready."

"That kid was born ready. If it comes down to her, I'd bet on her."

Linda watched as the next girl whiffed on her shot. Linda was shaking as she stepped to the spot. Linda's shot was heading for the goal when the other team's keeper dove flicking the shot off the post to save it. 2-2.

The next girls on each team made their shots. It would come down to Marie and her equal number on the other team. Up stepped the very confident leader of the opposing team. She took a booming shot that hit the crossbar and bounced back. The girl fell to her knees in disbelief. It now came down to Marie. Marie silently prayed as she approached the penalty spot. No one said a word. Marie knew what was on the line with the shot. Marie spotted the ball, took a deep breath and shot. Marie had her eyes closed, but she knew that it was good. Her teammates pig-piled on her screaming in joy. 3-2. Roadrunners win. The team went over to shake hands and thank the refs. Sam and Mac brought up the rear in the line. Everyone of the Roadrunners hugged the tear stained leader of the opposition. The teams had left it all on the field.

"Coach, that was one hell of a game. I hope the next time is just as exciting."

"Sam, we will win one of these games with you, someday." The men embraced and went back to gather their teams.

"That was one of the best games that I've ever played in or coached. I'm proud of you. Practice on Tuesday. Pickup your stuff and carry the gear to my car." Parents and players were happily milling around talking about the game. Mac moved over to Sam.

"The Chief and the county police have our friends surrounded. They are over by our cars."

"Okay, Mac. Let's make sure that all of the players and fans get away before we go to the cars." Sam and Mac watch as players and parents take the gear and set it by the car. Marie has moved over to Jude's car. Most of the team is congregating there. As Sam and Mac start heading to their cars; the police seem to be circling the wagons around the area.

"Coach, I need to talk to you." Scooter seemed to not notice the people around the car.

"Okay, talk."

"For years, you've been messing in my business. I'm here to tell you that it has to end."

"Scooter, that might be the dumbest thing that has ever come out of your mouth. I hadn't set eyes on you for over a decade. I never knew that Buddy died under strange circumstances. I'd say that Coben is the one you should be angry with, but he's dead. Along with Jones, Layton and almost my ex-wife. Whatever you're doing has nothing to do with me."

"Simone, you can't talk to Scooter that way." An angry priest started towards Sam with malice in his heart. Out of the blue another angry priest leveled Father Brody.

"And you can't threaten my friend." Eugene stood over the prone priest.

Scooter's friends and hired help started to leave when the police did their job. The group was soon controlled. The warrants were served on Scooter's cohorts.

"Simone, I'm not finished with you and your ilk. When you coached us, you turned my friends away from me. We had big plans, but you divided us. Coben held us together. Some of the guys got so bad that they had to go. Now, all these years later, you're keeping me from becoming rich beyond my dreams. I will get my revenge."

"Scooter, you need help. Do you think that you'll ever see another day of freedom? All of these killings and illegal business deals will keep you and your little band in prison for a long time." Scooter tried to break free from the officer that had him, but to no avail.

"Mr. Floyd, we have enough physical evidence and testimony from your sister to put all of you away for a long time." The County Sheriff deputy's words hit Scooter hard.

"That bitch, she has ruined me." Scooter slumped over in shock. Tad Shipley was loudly sobbing. Father Brody was starting to come around. Father Eugene leaned over the prone priest.

"The Archbishop sends his regards. He has suspended you from your duties as a priest. He wishes you the best, but will not raise a hand to help you."

Sam, Mac, Chief Petty, and Tim watched Scooter's group being loaded into vans to be transported to the county jail. Father Eugene soon joined the group.

"I had to talk to my boss. He has reappointed me as pastor of Blessed Family. I have a ten-year contract."

"Well, something good has come out of this mess. I might even come to Mass once in a while."

"That would be a true miracle." Everyone laughed breaking the tension.

"From what I understand, that when they moved on the Floyd's house, Cindy started talking and gave more information than the task force had. I don't have all the details, but she implicated them in crimes and murders going back to Buddy Johnson." Chief Petty shook his head as he thought about how dangerous and crazy the Floyds were.

"Now, you know why I didn't accept their offer to adopt me. I had seen enough to figure that no one was going to get out of there alive." The group turned to look at Tavin.

"This all started back when I coached you guys? I don't understand what happened in the short time that I coached the team for Scooter to have even started down this road."

"At that time, he was into stealing and building his private army. He picked kids that didn't have strong families. He gave them a look into a world of money and power. Scooter's parents were gone a lot. Scooter and Cindy spent money and time on enticing people into their inner circle. They loved doing more risky games as they got more people involved. When you coached us, it showed us an alternative to strive for. I have to admit that I took the money to go to school. I am a hypocrite. I still feel guilty. One thing I'm not is a criminal." Tavin turned and walked away.

THE CONCLUSION

Mac and Sam watched as the police left with Scooter and his gang. The parking lot was nearly empty. Jack Petty returned from talking to his men.

"Sam, Mac, I've got to head to the station to talk to my men. I'll let you know what is going on with the suspects. I'm glad that no one got hurt. That is a plus for our side." Sam nodded to Mac and climbed into his car.

"Jude, can we stop at the hospital on the way home?" Marie was staring out the side window as she asked.

"Sure, do you want me to come in?"

"Yes, I think that I need my mom with me." They were silent, except for David's non-stop chattering. Somehow, this gave them comfort.

"What floor is she on?"

"Third floor, room 315." They waited for an elevator. The wait and ride were short, but seemed to last forever. The three got off and headed to room 315. Marie looked inside the room. It was empty.

"There isn't anyone in there."

"Maybe, she's up and walking." A nurse walked by.

"Excuse me, but where is the patient in this room?"

"I don't know. You can check at the nurse's station." She pointed back towards the elevators.

"Thank You." The group turned around and retraced their steps.

"Hello, where is Jane Jones?"

"Are you family?" Marie Nodded. "Well, she was there at breakfast, but when we returned to check on her, she was gone."

"Gone, what do you mean gone?" Marie and Jude started to get bad feelings.

"She left with her clothes and walked out without anyone noticing."

"Oh my gosh! Was she well enough to leave?" Marie was on the verge of hysterics.

"Let me get the ward supervisor. She can answer your questions." Another nurse soon approached Jude and Marie.

"Hi, I'm Sue Benn, the floor supervisor. How can I help you?"

"I'm Jude Simone and this is Marie. Can you explain how Marie's mother Jane Jones could walk out unnoticed just days after being shot? We want to know what is or isn't being done to make sure that Jane is okay."

"First of all, we don't know what happened. The authorities removed the guard from her room last night and after breakfast this morning she was gone. We notified the police and searched the building. Ms. Jones was healing very well from her wounds, but could have a serious setback if she tries to do too much. You're her daughter, Marie."

"Yes, but she left a long time ago. This was the first time that I've seen her in years."

"How are you involved in this?" The supervisor turned towards Jude.

"I'm Marie's step-mother. We stopped to see Jane after Marie's soccer game."

"I can't promise much, but if you'll give me some information, I'll try to keep you informed if we hear anything."

"Thank you, that should help." The information was exchanged. Jude and Marie left the hospital and headed home.

The cab dropped the woman off at the corner. The woman looked around as if she was unsure of what to do. Finally, she made a decision and started walking down the alley. She came to a stop at a detached garage. Looking around before opening the door. Inside was an older Ford Escort. The woman grabbed some articles from the shelves and got in the car. She moved the car outside before relocking the garage door. She drove off.

The Simone's converged on their house from different directions. Not much was said in either car as they made their way home. Sam felt that the troubles of the last few weeks were at an end, but the looks on Jude and Marie's faces told him that they were not quite over.

"What's wrong?"

"We stopped at the hospital to check on Jane. She wasn't there."

"What do you mean, wasn't there?"

"She left. Gone without a word. She pulled a Jane on us again." Marie started crying.

"Sam, the hospital said that she disappeared between breakfast and lunch."

David put his little arms around his sister. Soon, all the Simone's were hugging Marie.

The rest of the weekend went by sort of quiet and dull. Dulled by the sadness that Marie and Joey were feeling over Jane's sudden appearance and departure.

Sam was up early on Monday morning. It was going to be a busy week at Good Sam's. The morning was filled with the normal sounds of the Simone house. A quick breakfast and kisses shoved Sam out the door. The T-Bird swept him to Good Sam's. Linda and Bob were already at work. Sam was making his way to his office. "Sam, line one is for you."

"Thanks, Linda. I'll get it in my office."

Sam sat down at his desk before picking up the phone. "Hello, Sam speaking."

"Sam, its me. I needed to call you, especially after my abrupt departure."

"Okay, speak Jane. You're not high on my list right now."

"Oh Sam, I never meant to hurt the kids again, but I needed to get lost. That's no excuse. Also, I wanted to thank you for saving me. As always, you came through. Thanks Sam." The line went dead.

Printed in Great Britain
by Amazon